# HARD CASE

## ALICE WHITE INVESTIGATOR BOOK TWO

MARC HIRSCH

Oct 15, 2021

Dear Nancy,
This was inspired
by dad's childhood
in Hell's Kitchen,
Marc (Hirsch)

Printed in the United States of America

First Printing, 2018

ISBN 978-1984371195

www.marchirsch.com

# TABLE OF CONTENTS

# CHAPTER 1

## NIGHT

In the 1500s, the Lenape Indians traveled and fished the waterways of New York Harbor. Four centuries later, the harbor had become the site of the bustling Port of New York and New Jersey.

A dense fog hung over the water. Waves slapped the piers. The smell of seawater and tar penetrated the night air. Thick lines groaned under the strain of ships at dock. Tugs tended their floating trusts. In the final hours of the night, the port sat at rest, protecting its living organism of cargo and crew.

At rest, but certainly not asleep.

The spring temperature was mild, but the young man shook as if it were polar winter. His hands trembled violently as he lit his last cigarette. He crushed the empty package and tossed it into the breeze. He leaned into the chain-link fence against which he had been thrown. He lifted his battered face to the stars. Through his broken glasses, they sparkled like diamonds on a jeweler's cloth.

The night air seeped through his broken nose. The taste of beer mingled with his blood.

He took a deep drag on the cigarette, only vaguely aware of the two men standing in front of him. One of them held a gun pointed at his forehead. They were shadows, phantoms, ghosts in the moonlight.

The finger whitened on the trigger.

His being merged with his surroundings—the docks, the sea, the gulls, the sky overhead.

Somewhere inside him was an ethereal presence, an island of tranquility he had been aware of since he was a small child, a dream-self he felt certain would survive this night even though he was positive his mortal body would not.

Alice White's boyfriend, Jim Peters, was still asleep in her apartment on the west side of the six-lane boulevard known as the Grand Concourse in the Bronx, New York City. It may not have been the standard of behavior for a single woman in 1956. Still, she was pleased with their relationship and had no intention of further committing herself, despite his obvious wish for her to do so. One failed marriage for each of them was enough to last a lifetime, she thought.

It was a sunny morning in May. Alice put on her favorite pair of gym shorts, rubber-banded her straight black hair, and ran north up the Concourse toward Jerome Avenue. She was thirty-five years old with curves in all the right places. She was not only superficially pretty, but her assertive nature rendered her incredibly attractive to some men, intimidating to others. Jim liked to think of himself as self-confident, but Alice strained his nerves to their limit.

She had graceful, athletic legs. A woman running bare-legged on the public streets, for anyone to see, was yet another deviation from society's norms. She honestly did not care. She was running in the footsteps of her idol, the "flying housewife," Fanny Blankers-Koen, who had won four gold medals at the 1948 Summer Olympics in London. If it was okay for Fanny, it was good enough for her.

Alice made her way north, up the sidewalk, under the el on Jerome Avenue, until she got to Zabronski's Meats.

The sawdust on the floor and the smell of fresh-cut meat always made her mouth water in anticipation of Zabronski's perfect steaks and chops on her table.

"What can I get for you this beautiful morning, young lady?" the short, ebullient, mostly bald-headed butcher asked Alice in his thick European accent. He had been liberated from a concentration camp at the end of the war. His protuberant belly and multiple gold-capped teeth were the results of his nonstop celebration of freedom in the decade since. Alice had met his lovely wife and delightful daughter on previous visits to the shop.

Her answer to Mr. Zabronski was lost in the deafening screech of metal on metal as a train passed overhead.

When the train was gone, she repeated, "Mr. Zabronski, I am dying for some of your lamb chops. Would you cut me six, please?"

"Six? Aha. You have company. It wouldn't be that good-looking young man you were in here with a couple of weeks ago, would it? You like him, huh? The way he looks at you, I'd say he's a good one, and very polite too."

Alice was amused that everyone was "young" to Mr. Zabronski, and "good-looking," "handsome," or "pretty." She enjoyed the fact that he liked Jim. Mr. Z was in his sixties, but he had a sadness and a stare in his eyes that made him seem much older. He had told her of his captivity and his terror in the camps. He would never lose that look, it seemed to her. She could only imagine the cruelty he had been subjected to. The thick-shouldered butcher was the classic immigrant the Statue of Liberty was meant to welcome.

Alice watched Mr. Zabronski deftly cut her chops from a rack of lamb. He was a surgeon in a bloodstained white apron. She took money out of her pocket as he finished wrapping the meat in butcher paper and tied the package with string. He made the change for her from his ancient cash register.

"Thank you, Mr. Zabronski. Say hello to your family for me."

"Be well, young lady. Enjoy your lamb."

Alice stepped onto the sidewalk and

spotted an acne-pocked teenage boy sprinting toward her with a lady's handbag under his arm. A young woman was running after him, yelling, "Stop! Stop! Give me back my purse! Help, somebody. He stole my purse!"

Alice put her foot out and sent the boy, face-first, onto the pavement. She grabbed the purse.

Mr. Zabronski appeared in the doorway of his shop, brandishing a knife. He looked to be considering carving the thief into pieces. He glared at the fallen man. The kid stood up, sneering back through his bleeding face at Alice, Zabronski, and the woman whose purse he had taken, obviously contemplating an attack to retrieve his prize. Zabronski shook his knife at him and surveyed the kid's face. It would take weeks to heal.

Alice glared back at the enraged teenager and told him, "Yeah, that's right. Two women and a butcher. You think you can take us?"

The boy reconsidered, turned, and fled up the hill empty-handed, away from the pretty but insane woman and her two companions.

"I DIDN'T THINK SO!" Alice yelled after him.

"That was so nice of you, and so brave too," the sandy-haired woman told Alice. "I can't thank you enough. My name is Susan Atkins. Please, let me buy you a cup of coffee."

Alice handed Susan her purse. "Okay. Sure, but I can't stay long. I have to get this meat home. I have company."

Alice then turned to Mr. Zabronski and told him, "Thanks for the backup, Mr. Zabronski. As always, the perfect gentleman."

"It didn't look to me like you needed any backup, young lady. You're a credit to your sex. This'll be a great advertisement for the business. I can see the headline: 'Purse Snatcher Foiled by Gorgeous Young Lady Customer Of Zabronski's Fabulous Butcher Shop! 'Come by next time your boyfriend is in town, and I'll cut you some nice steaks on the house."

"What a great idea for publicity, Mr. Z. It just so happens I have a friend at the *Post*, a reporter named Franklin Jones. I think I'll give him a call and see if he'll run it. This'll put me in solid with my bosses downtown. They love hearing about me risking my life to thwart crime. It's their peculiar form of entertainment. Who knows, it might bring in business for you and us both."

# CHAPTER 2

## LADIES OF THE CONCOURSE

There is nothing like springtime in New York City. The month of May has those mild temperatures and that clean new foliage that apartment dwellers look forward to all winter long. They can finally go outside without jackets or coats, and, most wonderfully, women are back in skirts and sleeveless blouses.

It was late on a weekday afternoon. High above the sidewalk in front of Alice's building hung the annual green canopy of branches growing from the precisely spaced oak trees lining both sides of the impressive Grand Concourse. Finished in 1909, modeled after the Champs-Élysées in Paris, the

Concourse spans the entire four-mile length of the borough of the Bronx.

After a gray winter of snow and frigid temperatures, Alice was happy to be out of doors, conversing with her neighbor, Elaine Applewood. She'd bought a folding beach chair at Woolworth's the year before.

Alice sat in a skirt, with her legs crossed, watching the traffic. A cigarette she had accepted from Elaine dangled from her lips. It was a Kent with the "micronite filter," theoretically less unhealthy than any other cigarette on the market.

"Thanks," Alice told Elaine. "I'm trying to stop, but smoking is just so relaxing. Anyway, it's too beautiful to quit today. They say these filters are actually good for your health."

Elaine was three years younger than Alice, with legs that drove passing strangers and delivery boys wild, especially in spring when they had been deprived of the sight for so long. They were shown off nicely by her pink cotton dress. Her brown hair was cut short in the manner of the other female staff in her office. She was an executive secretary for the president of an auto parts company not far south, on Fordham Road. Her husband, Harry, was a United States Customs officer, somewhat older than she was, but who nonetheless took excellent care of her personal needs. Besides his attention in the bedroom, his job afforded her some very expensive clothing, perfume, jewelry, and home furnishings. She had no complaints.

Elaine took a puff on her own cigarette, rolled her eyes at Alice, and replied, "I don't actually believe that. I think it's just a rumor they started to sell cigarettes. I think they're bad for you no matter what kind of filter they have."

Elaine and Harry Applewood would have personified the happy post–World War II American couple had they had any children, but they did not. They had tried and failed. They agreed that half the fun was trying. Both seemed perfectly happy without offspring.

"You know, Alice," Elaine mused, "it's

eleven years since the War ended. I still can't get over having meat on the table whenever we want it. We ate a lot of spaghetti during the War. I still make Harry spaghetti once a week, for old times 'sake."

Elaine's words sounded chatty and cheerful enough, but Alice could tell something was bothering her.

Alice inquired, "Is something the matter, Elaine?"

Elaine looked back at Alice, took in a breath, raised her eyebrows as if to speak, but changed her mind and answered with forced nonchalance, "Not really. Same old stuff, nothing's new."

Something was definitely up with Elaine, but this was New York City, and one could easily bring unnecessary chaos into one's life by sticking one's nose into other people's business. Alice had demonstrated this to herself repeatedly.

The conversation was brought to a halt by the arrival of their neighbor Brenda

Montgomery and her two kids. Brenda noticed the Kents and waved her filterless Pall Mall at them, announcing, “If you’re going to die, you might as well do it with one of these babies.”

They all laughed.

Brenda’s two kids had just gotten home from being bossed around by teachers all day and were not interested in further contact with adults, so they moved away from the women to play further up the block.

“Kids,” Brenda told them, “don’t go too far.”

They shook their heads up and down.

“Well, girls, how’re you two doing?”

“Just great, Brenda,” Alice responded. “Life is good. Jim quit building houses upstate after his ordeal last year. He went back to working on Broadway. Right now, he’s in Manhattan taking care of the set of *My Fair Lady*. He supervised its construction before it opened a couple of months ago. How are things with you?”

"Just peachy, Alice. I got the kids and Walter up this morning, made them breakfast, made the kids 'lunches, cleaned the apartment, did the laundry, flipped through magazines, drank lots of wine, smoked lots of Pall Malls, grocery shopped, flirted with the delivery boy, got most of tonight's dinner together so I don't have to do much when I go back upstairs, washed the martini pitcher, and made sure there was plenty of ice. The lot of a housewife in the 1950s is a living dream."

Brenda cleared her face of escaped strands of the blond hair she had tried to pin out of her way. She was quite pretty when she wasn't complaining. Before leaving her apartment, she had downed several large glasses of wine to celebrate this break in her daily routine.

"Alice, you ought to give marriage another try," Brenda told her neighbor. "It's fabulous." She rolled her eyes skyward.

"Please, Brenda. I tried it. I really did. Andy and I had a very physical relationship, if you know what I mean. We were two very attractive people if I do say so, and very compatible that way. Unfortunately, when we were fully dressed, there was no respect. We were at odds in every area of our life. We were both very self-centered, selfish, immature, dishonest, and inconsiderate. I am not willing to give those qualities up for any man, so I swore off serious relationships for the rest of my life. That was my solution."

"Gee, Alice. I'd kill for a purely physical relationship," Brenda responded. "Are you kidding? I hope you don't think this is too personal. But I can't remember the last time Walter satisfied me in bed. He gets what he wants, rolls over, and falls asleep."

"God," Elaine chimed in. "Are you sure you want to be telling us that kind of intimate detail, Brenda?"

"Well, aren't you Miss Goody Two-Shoes, Elaine," Brenda questioned, "all prim and proper? I'll bet Harry is a tiger in bed. As long as we're being completely honest with each other, you want to tell us if I'm right?"

"What do you mean 'we, 'Brenda?"

Alice came to Elaine's defense. "You're the one being open and, to tell you the truth, that was much more than I wanted to know about you and Walter."

"I'm sorry, Alice, and you too, Elaine. It's just that I'm locked in the house all day, with nothing exciting to do but fantasize about lewd encounters with strange men and drink wine. If I accidentally bump into a piece of furniture, I go off like a firecracker. That's how keyed up I am. You girls have lives outside your apartments. I only get to talk about these things with other women when I get a chance and fantasize about them when I'm alone. I was out of line. I'm sorry."

Elaine felt bad for Brenda, so she offered, "Harry is good in bed. That's all the detail I'm willing to offer on the subject. I do sympathize with you, though, Brenda. I'm just not comfortable talking about those kinds of things. That's the way I was brought up. You know, it's not all a bed of roses. We haven't been able to have kids for some reason. And Harry's having trouble at work, and he's drinking more than usual. He's depressed, but he won't tell me what it's about. I'm going out of my mind worrying about him. Is that enough honesty? Sex isn't everything. Okay, Alice, it's your turn."

"Who said I wanted a turn, Elaine? What makes you think I would be willing to talk about the intimate details of my life with you? I will say they're good, but I don't trust it would stay that way long if Jim and I got married. What do you think, Brenda? It sounds like you have the kind of regrets I'm looking to avoid."

"Nice, Alice, using me as your expert on marriage. You have to be kidding. I fell in love with Walter's uniform when he was on leave from the Pacific. He was never trained to take care of a woman romantically. I've tried to instruct him, but he accuses me of picking on him, so I just gave up, and I trade his use of my body for food, clothing, and a roof over the kids 'heads. I think we've passed the point of no return. I don't think it'll ever get any better. I have to take care of my own personal satisfaction, you know?"

"God, Brenda," Alice exclaimed, "it sounds so grim. Why do you stay with him?"

"Alice, you're so naive. He's not a bad man, and he's a good father to Julie and Joey. I don't know where you get these ideas about relationships. You know, though, I do admire your nerve, running down the street half-naked. You're killing the neighborhood women. Their husbands stop talking when you run by in your shorts with those legs. It makes me jealous too."

"I'm sorry if it offends anyone," Alice shot back, "but that's the trade-off for being single. I need to burn off the stress of the day. You should try it, Brenda."

"Yeah, sure, Alice. Walter would have a seizure if I put those shorts on and headed out. Either that or he'd tear the shorts off my body before I made it to the door and have his way with me. I don't want to give him any more of those kinds of ideas. He gets enough of them on his own."

"I was fine being single and by myself," Alice told them. "I worked with lawyers during the day and went to NYU Law School at night. I took the train to Madison Square Garden for the fights on Saturday nights and caught baseball games at the Stadium when the Yankees were in town. Everything was just fine until I met Jim Peters and traveled up the Hudson to get him out of trouble. He was wrongly accused of killing some doctor due to faulty construction of a house. I must have lost my mind. He annoyed me, wore un-ironed shirts, his teeth were white and straight. He built his own houses, and he lived so much better upstate than I did down here in the city. It depressed me, and I resented him. Everything about him bothered me. I felt more like his spinster sister than an attractive woman, and I blamed him for making me feel that way. Then one night, I went to the refrigerator in a shirt and underwear, and he came out and saw me and was struck dumb. I don't think I was consciously out to seduce him, but I can't be certain. Anyway, it was like taking candy from a baby. He was mine, all mine. I couldn't resist the temptation. It's his problem, not mine. Maybe I should have worn slacks that night. I don't know. Now I can't get rid of him. I can't stop grinning at him either. Neither can he. It's humiliating. I'm not marrying anyone that I can't defend myself against. I don't like being that vulnerable."

"You're not doing anything to relieve my jealousy, Alice," Brenda commented. "Maybe you're right to stay single. As I said, I'm no great expert. I've pretty much made a mess of my life, except for the kids. They are worth everything."

"Now it's my turn to be jealous of you, Brenda," Elaine told her. "I have wanted a baby for so long, but nothing's happened. We talked about adoption, but we're just not ready to throw in the towel."

Having talked themselves out, the ladies sat in silence, content, released from the troubles of the day, their cares vanishing in the fine spring afternoon.

The screech of tires on pavement ended their separate reveries. A driver fixated on the three pairs of beautiful legs on the sidewalk to his right suddenly became aware that the car in front of him had stopped for a red light.

The spell was broken. The three women giggled at the accident their stunning selves had almost caused. They had each been in their own world and were now aware of the sounds of traffic on the street in front of them. The light turned green, and the cars departed. A bus lumbered by, gears grinding, extruding a black cloud of exhaust on its way to Fordham Road and points south.

"Well, it's time for me to head up and see what my choices are for dinner," Alice announced.

Brenda Montgomery commented, "I envy you, Alice, cooking for one. It's time for me to get dinner together for the four of us and whip up a pitcher of martinis for my hubby. He'd better not be late, or the pitcher will be gone.

"JOEY! JULIE!" she called. "Time to

get ready for supper. Come say goodbye to Miss White and Mrs. Applewood."

Joey and Julie ran over and politely said goodbye to the women, then left with their mother.

With that, Alice and Elaine picked up their things and headed into the building.

"Anytime you want to talk, Elaine, let me know," Alice told her.

"I will," Elaine replied. "Thanks. I mean it. I might give you a call sometime."

*That'll be the day*, Alice thought.

# CHAPTER 3

## BURGLARY

Alice got off the elevator and headed for her apartment to consider what to have for dinner. With Jim in her life, the refrigerator and cabinets offered a variety she was not used to. Still, she might have to pick up something from the grocery store after she dropped off her beach chair and took inventory.

She propped the folding chair against the wall next to her door. Then she unlocked the top lock and flipped to the next key for the bottom lock. She turned the knob, pushed in just slightly on the metal door, and saw the coat closet was wide open. She remembered closing its door securely on her way out. Without crossing the threshold, she knew she was being robbed. She opened the door to the full extent of her arm and yanked it closed as hard and as fast as she could. The crash of the slamming door was ear-shattering. Before the reverberations had ceased, and before anyone inside her apartment could overtake her, Alice launched herself down the staircase to the left of her apartment entrance. She made it to the next landing in a single bound and swung herself into a half turn, using the landing post, to the floor below. In this manner, as she had done many times as a child in Queens, using the post at the end of each banister, she made it all the way down to the lobby. Once there, she bolted through the mirrored, marble-floored art deco lobby and out to the sidewalk. She raced down the block, across 205th Street, and into Harrison's corner drugstore.

She fought to control her breathing. She walked to the back of the pharmacy, opened the accordion door of the phone booth, dropped a dime in the slot, and rotated the dial to zero.

"Hello, operator," she said, "give me the police." The phone rang in her ears like something out of a black-and-white crime drama.

From the time of her marriage to Andy Matthews, a uniformed officer of the NYPD, Alice recognized one of his friends, Artie Johnson, when he arrived in response to her call.

"Here are my keys, Artie." She told him her apartment number and handed him the keys, then waited in the pharmacy for him and his partner to secure her place.

When it was all clear, she entered and saw that all three of her electrical appliances—the used table radio, her record player, and the toaster—had been wrapped in their cords and placed on top of her kitchen table. The drawers of her bedroom bureau were pulled open and the contents dumped on the floor. She had nothing of value hidden in them, even amongst her underwear. It was sad how little she owned worth stealing. She didn't have a television set. She went through the apartment and discovered the only thing missing was the expensive gold pendulum clock her mentally unstable cousin, Stanley, had mailed to each of his relatives six months earlier from Switzerland during one of his manic episodes. It never did keep the correct time. Her mother, Rose, and her Aunt Betsy had been unable to get theirs to keep the correct time either.

In the kitchen, she told Artie, "I hope whoever stole that clock has better luck getting it to work than I did."

Artie smiled at her. "I'm impressed you were smart enough not to bust in here and try to take these guys on. I know you can get crazy when someone crosses you. These thieves have been around the Bronx for a couple of weeks now. They already stabbed two of the people who interrupted them. We have been chasing them all over. We'll get 'em."

Alice's face reddened in irritation.

"You could have been hurt," Artie went on. "We'll check the pawnshops for your clock, but don't hold your breath."

"What'd you mean by that remark about me getting crazy, Artie?"

"Ugh. Geez. I'm sorry, Alice. No offense, but Andy and I are still friends and, with a few beers in him, he sometimes talks about you. If it's any consolation, I think he's still got a thing for you, but please, if you see him, do not tell him I said that."

Alice checked the depths of her kitchen cabinets, which Jim Peters had helped her fill. She found the new Browning .380 automatic that her friend and protector, Antonio Vargas, had insisted she buy to replace the one of dubious origin he had lent her on their adventure together a year earlier. It was in its original box, unopened.

The story about Antonio was a long

one, but she had happened on a robbery in progress and saved Antonio's life just before traveling upstate to help Jim Peters, one of her boss's friends.

Shortly after that, during her investigation into Jim's troubles, attempts were made on her life, the first of which was close enough for her to swallow her pride and call Antonio for help. He responded immediately. There had been considerable physical tension between them, but it was never consummated. Initially, they had put it aside to take care of the business at hand. Then she got involved with Jim, and Antonio got engaged to Maria, who later became his wife. So she and Vargas were just friends with other romantic entanglements. Even so, he had a proprietary interest in her living a long and healthy life.

He would certainly insist on training her to use her gun when he heard about this break-in.

Alice pulled open the junk drawer in the kitchen where she stored screwdrivers, pliers, twine, etc. In it she found the pristine, still-sealed box of .380 cartridges she had placed there. CARTUGES HECHO EN MEXICO was stamped in black ink on the side.

Wasn't it enough that Antonio had told her to expect a bang when she squeezed the trigger? She got it. How much more was there to learn about using a gun? Now, that would not be enough for either Antonio or Jim. They would intimidate her into becoming competent with the weapon she both feared and despised for its ability to kill.

A few days after the burglary, Alice and Jim were together in her apartment. She buzzed Frankie, her window washer, into the building for his regular visit. He did the windows for many of her neighbors and people in buildings up and down the Concourse. With the black smoke and visible ash from incinerators and the chemical fog that hung over the Bronx, tenants who could afford it requested Frankie's service every couple of weeks so they could get a clearer look at the world from inside their apartments. For days after a visit from Frankie, Alice would marvel at the clarity with which she was able to view her slice of the city.

"Frankie the window washer" was a Bronx fixture. A wiry Italian in his seventies, his head and face were skeletal. His perpetual impish grin was missing several teeth. His eyes danced like candle flames through ellipses cut above a picket-fence smile. His skull sat just like a jack-o'-lantern on his shoulders. City window washers wore a skull cap as part of their uniform. Frankie's was made of gray suede that matched his vest. The string of his tobacco pouch hung from the front pocket, and a lit, hand-rolled cigarette very often dangled from his mouth.

Frankie had been an aerialist of the city's fire escapes since his youth, climbing the tenements of Little Italy in Manhattan. He loved talking to the young children who lived in the homes on his route about his life and times. They all knew the story of his lovely wife, whom he believed had been an Indian princess in a previous incarnation. The kids were mesmerized by him. It was such a treat if they were lucky enough to be home from school when he showed up to wash their apartment windows. With his romantic stories and homespun advice, he had a dramatic impact on their young lives. They would never forget him.

Frankie was excited and disturbed by Alice's report of the break-in and robbery. She told him she never wanted to see that gold pendulum clock again, that she was glad it was gone. Neither she nor the cops understood how the thief or thieves had gotten into her place. The two heavy front door locks had not been tampered with. They could have used a rope from the roof down to the open bathroom window, but that seemed way too far, too dangerous, and highly unlikely.

She introduced Frankie to Jim. They shook hands.

Frankie winked and grinned at Alice. "Nice-looking guy," he wheezed.

Jim flushed.

Alice led the window washer down the hallway to her bedroom, where the apartment's only fire escape protruded off the rear of the building. Jim trailed behind, fascinated by this colorful Bronx character. Frankie climbed out onto the black wrought iron fire escape. He looked back and smiled at the happy couple watching him. Then, like a magician on the stage, he snatched the tobacco pouch out of his vest pocket with two fingers, tapped some of its contents onto a white paper, rolled a cigarette with one hand, licked the paper, lit it, and dropped the match to the pavement far below.

While they were marveling at his dexterity, without warning, Frankie placed his foot up onto the edge of the fire escape railing and raised himself to a full stand. There he remained balanced on one foot as if on a high wire above the Grand Canyon. Alice almost retched in fear for Frankie's life. Several feet from the bedroom window fire escape was the bathroom window, unlatched and swung wide open on its vertical hinges for ventilation, now resting against the side of the building. It was unreachable from the fire escape, so she'd thought it was safe to leave it open all day. Jim was enthralled, but it did not escape his notice that he had stopped breathing. Alice had too much respect for Frankie to beg him to come down. She was transfixed by the prospect of Frankie falling to his death.

When the tension could not get any greater, Frankie leaped off the fire escape onto the bathroom windowsill.

"This is how they got in," he rasped back at his terrified audience.

Alice promised herself never to leave the bathroom window unlatched again.

Unknown to his customers, Frankie "Windows" Amato had only begun his window-washing route through the Bronx after retiring from a life of crime. Washing windows was meditative work. It kept his aerial skills sharp and put some change in his pocket. The tips were good, and he orchestrated a little sideline. He assessed the contents of the apartments he serviced. On occasion, at his direction, and only with his permission, he would have his small crew of second-story men relieve a customer of their valuables to supplement their mutual incomes.

Alice White was a favorite of his, and he had given neither instruction nor permission to steal from her.

Frankie finished Alice's windows, said goodbye, and headed to a phone booth to cancel the rest of his jobs for the day. His crew had gotten out of hand. He would have to straighten them out.

*I'm getting too old for this shit*, he thought.

# CHAPTER 4

## THE GUN STORE

Irish Pete and Scar leaned against the wall of the alley alongside the warehouse. Each smoked a Lucky Strike in silence. Pete was six foot four and 260 pounds of solid muscle. On his dusky face was a scowl that froze men in their tracks. His chest was massive. Despite his brutish look, he was the intellect of the pair. Guys he knew told him he thought too much. Scar was a couple of inches shorter with a lighter complexion and a smile on his face. He carried his mass at a much lower center of gravity. He got his name from the thick welt that ran down his left cheek, a trophy from a knife fight as a teenager hanging around the waterfront. His hair was black and curly, his arms like tree trunks. In contrast to his partner, he was all brawn and no brains. He compensated for Pete's overthinking by not thinking at all. His protuberant belly and friendly disposition filled his opponents with false hope. His slovenly appearance concealed the force and capability for violence of a rogue elephant.

There was nothing on Scar's mind but the impending opportunity to scare the crap out of the man they had been sent to confront. They both wore dungarees and work boots. Pete's T-shirt was black with an auto parts logo on it. Scar's was blue with a beer ad on it. Black and blue. Appropriate.

They were longshoremen. They liked to think of themselves as Tillio and Truck, Johnny Friendly's thugs in "On the Waterfront." They'd sat through that movie, stuffing their faces with concession food, a bunch of times when it first came out a few years ago. The only difference was, they were for real. They weren't actors. Their boss made Johnny Friendly look like Whistler's mother.

No matter. This was going to be a simple job of brutality and intimidation: the dishing out of pain, specifically to the kidneys and stomach, the back and sides of the head, but not to the face, nothing lethal and nothing that required a hospital afterward. Those were their instructions. Careful words to the victim, after he was down, about how he could avoid this, or worse, in the future. That would be Pete's department. Scar wasn't so good with words.

Afterward, the two would slip over to Murphy's Bar for a couple of beers and a few shots of whiskey before returning to unloading cargo.

Life was sweet.

Irving Teleducci hated his name. For

God's sake, who would name their kid that? He guessed he was some mix of Dutch and Italian. He'd rarely seen his parents when they were alive, so he wasn't sure where they were from. They died when he was small. He'd bunked with various relatives as a kid but mainly grew up on the Manhattan docks. A "wharf rat." A homeless, orphaned kid with no place else to go.

Irving, it turned out, was a very bright young man. He read a lot and was good with numbers. But when he spoke, he sounded like Leo Gorcey, the Dead End Kid, with a thick, wise guy New York accent. It made him sound like less than the genius he was.

In his teens, Irving had been noticed around the docks by some of the dockworkers. They would give him a few bucks to run errands. He got them cigarettes, beer, and takeout. One of the union managers found out he was good with numbers and taught him double- and triple-entry bookkeeping. In a few years, he was keeping books for the powerful Dockworkers 'Union.

He was now twenty-eight years old.

Artie's Guns and Ammo was nestled in a quiet side street of Trenton, New Jersey. It was owned by Artie Canfield, a beefy, pockmarked man in his late forties, who tied his scraggly brown hair back in a ponytail. He smoked Camels and took swigs, throughout the day, from the bottle in the back room. Gregarious as he may have been, he was suspicious of strangers. He was far from a pillar of virtue himself, often exchanging merchandise with men of bad repute. Many of his customers were aware of this and counted on him for good deals.

Although it was a weekday morning in mid-spring, the store was not empty. Two men in gray shirts with business logos embroidered on them and matching pants, apparently on their way to work, looked longingly into Artie's glass cases at the array of handguns for sale. There were revolvers, automatics, pistols, and derringers. Colts, Remingtons, Smith & Wessons, Mausers, and Walthers. The men imagined firing them at intruders.

Artie pointed through the glass countertop and named the various weapons, talking about their history and which ones had distinguished themselves in combat or competition.

One of the men glanced at his watch and shook Artie's hand. "We'll be back," he told him, and they departed.

When the two had left, the young man who had been up front checking out rifles ambled over to the counter. Artie suspected the skinny, curly-haired kid with glasses was just some college boy fascinated by the world of firearms. With the store empty of other customers, he was happy to oblige.

"What can I do for you, young feller?"

"I'm interested in a revolver," the man said in as thick a Brooklyn accent as Artie had ever heard. “A Colt .357. I seen it in a gun magazine, and I liked the way it looked. D’ya sell many a them?” he asked.

Artie, always ready to chat about his merchandise, answered, “Yeah, they been pretty popular this year. At ninety dollars each, they’re out of many people’s range, but I still can’t keep enough of them in the display case. Here’s one.” He reached into a case and handed an unloaded gun to the stranger.

“Mighty nice,” Teleducci said, hefting the weapon, “but at ninety bucks, it’s outta my range too. I heard about a guy selling these for fifty bucks apiece on the waterfront.”

“Well, that sounds mighty interesting.” Artie raised his eyebrows. He pulled a pack of cigarettes out of his shirt pocket, shook one out, and placed an end in his mouth. “You don’t have any idea where he’s getting ’em from, do ya?”

The store owner patted his pockets, looking for matches, and came up empty-handed. The kid pulled a pack of matches out of his own pocket, struck one, and lit Artie up.

"No," he answered, "but I'm from around them docks. I could do some snooping and find out for you. If you're interested, gimme your number, and I'll get back to you."

"We're in business," Irving told his driver when he got back in the car.

# CHAPTER 5

## THE BEATING

Inspector Harry Applewood had put together his own private break room inside a warehouse a short walk from customs. The door had a lock and a backup bolt on the inside. Harry was a fixture on the docks. The longshoremen were used to seeing him duck into his little sanctuary for a nap on the cot or some reading at the old oak desk. It was dark inside and smelled of seaweed and mold. There was a work sink, the desk, a rickety wooden swivel chair, and a floor lamp. The cot was just a bare mattress on a frame. A piece of broken mirror was nailed on the wall so he could comb his hair before returning to the office. A brown plastic radio sat on the desk for music and baseball games.

Through the walls, Harry heard the sea and the muffled sounds of conversation from passing dockworkers.

He sat at the desk with his head in his hands, the jacket of his customs uniform open, shirt collar undone, and tie loosened. His full head of graying hair was disheveled. His skull throbbed, and his kidneys hurt from the beating he had just taken. There was blood in his urine.

A bottle of Scotch was open on the desk. The cap lay beside it. He sucked up the contents of a glass, swished some around in his mouth, swallowed, and took a drag on his cigarette, a Kent. His wife Elaine had insisted he switch to Kents from Camels because they were supposedly healthier. What a joke.

*Why me?* he asked himself. *I'm supposed to have guts. I proved that in the war. I must be getting soft. I folded like a cheap suit at the first threat to Elaine and me. I should have gotten her out of town and gone to the police. That's what they'll say when they catch me, and they will catch me. Of that, I have no doubt. I'm gonna lose my job and go to prison. There's not a person I can turn to. They'll know. They'll find out. They have people in the police department and spies inside customs.*

Harry thought his head was about to catch fire, what with the pain, the alcohol, and the depression. A handful of aspirin had no effect.

He capped the bottle and put it back into his desk. He stubbed out the cigarette and splashed his face with cold water. He ran a comb through his hair in front of the shard of mirror on the wall. At the door, he straightened his tie.

Harry stepped, squinting, out into the bright sunlight of the dock. When his eyes adjusted, he saw men gathering to unload the ship he was about to inspect. There was an anticipatory bustle of activity, cargo hooks and ropes being collected, blocks and tackles being brought out of the warehouse.

Strolling inconspicuously through the crowd was the despicable messenger, Irving Teleducci, the man who'd delivered the news that destroyed Harry's happy life. The threats and instructions that had begun his downward spiral as a United States Customs officer. The kid had clearly enjoyed the power he exerted over an educated, respected war hero and agent of the federal government.

Applewood tried to control his rage and frustration. This man was only a pathetic lackey, caught in the current of waterfront power just like he was. Harry tried to settle down. He talked to himself, remembered the danger he was in, but he could not forget how disrespectfully Teleducci had spoken to him about Elaine and himself. They would do things to her and make him watch if he didn't do what they said.

He knew better than to make a scene. He had boxed in the navy. He could destroy this young punk. Hitting the kid would be suicide. It would also be an act of cowardice. But the alcohol in Harry's system and the pain in his kidneys overrode his good judgment.

"Hey, you, moron," Harry yelled. The young man glanced up without acknowledging him. Men cleared a space between them.

Irving finally turned his head toward Harry, stared with pity at the inspector, and kept walking.

Harry was filled with rage. He lost all self-restraint.

Irving sped up to leave the poor customs guy behind. Applewood was in deep enough trouble without him adding to it by allowing this to become a confrontation.

In a few quick steps, Harry was on Teleducci. He grabbed his shoulder and spun him around.

"I'm talking to you, you son of a bitch!"

Then he punched the much younger and frailer man hard in the face, breaking his glasses and knocking him down. As if that was not enough, Harry bent down and punched him again.

Harry came to his senses, turned, and walked off. Irving sat on the dock, trying to stop the bleeding from the cut under his eye with his sleeve.

*This is not good*, Irving thought. *I hate being stuck in the middle of it. My eye is gonna blacken, and the boss will ask me what happened.*

Men had stopped and were staring at him. One of them gave Irving a handkerchief and a hand up. Even if he wanted to protect the sorry bastard, Irving couldn't lie about it. Everyone in creation would know the truth.

Inspector Applewood was in deep trouble.

# CHAPTER 6

## NOONER

The next day Harry could not focus on work. He was as depressed as he had ever been. If things weren't bad enough, he had beaten up the messenger and sealed his, and maybe his wife's, fate. All that was left was to await retribution. If they didn't shoot him, he might die of fright.

He mostly avoided discussing work with Elaine, especially this latest display of poor judgment, but she would have to be completely unconscious not to be aware of the stress he was under. He feared that he had put her in grave danger. He hoped that, whatever they were planning for him, they would leave her alone, but he couldn't take that chance. He had to get her out of town.

"Hi, Elaine," Harry said when he called her from his desk while she was working in the Bronx. "I'm sorry to disturb you in the middle of the morning. Listen, I'm sure you're aware I'm having problems at work. It would be a great help if I knew you were safely out of town. Do you think you could take a leave of absence from your job? See if you can arrange that. We'll talk more tonight at home. Okay? I love you. Bye."

Harry inspected the cargo of the Spanish freighter, which required his personal attention. Then he made a beeline for his little room and finished off the remainder of the bottle of whiskey. He broke the seal of another and poured as much down his gullet as he could swallow before choking.

He was disgusted with himself. No way could he go back to work. He'd do the paperwork tomorrow. He headed directly for the train to the Bronx without stopping at his office.

"Hello, Phil," Harry spoke into the receiver of a pay phone near the station. "I won't be coming back to work today. Something's come up," he told his subordinate customs inspector, Philip Madison.

Something had come up. His breakfast lay in a puddle on the sidewalk next to the booth.

He hit the steps into the station.

The life he had been living was over. He was still breathing, but that could change at any moment. He imagined how this would play out if he lived. Disgraced, he would rot in prison, maybe north up the Hudson River at Sing Sing Prison. Thank goodness he and Elaine had not been able to have children. His sister, Nancy, would have to live with the shame.

He was on borrowed time. On the off chance the union boss, Menken, would forgive his temporary insanity, he would return to work tomorrow and keep doing what he was told. If he behaved, he never knew, they might let it go. After all, they needed him.

At Bedford Park in the Bronx, Harry climbed the stairs and stepped onto the Grand Concourse. He gave a sickly smile of acknowledgment to the newsie, Jimmy, in his green wooden shed. Harry's stomach was still queasy. He expected it would stay that way for the rest of what was left of his life. He felt a little tipsy but managed the two blocks to his apartment building.

As he rounded the corner into the dirty white brick building's front courtyard, he suddenly encountered his neighbor, Brenda Montgomery, and banged heads with her.

"Ouch. You almost knocked me out," Brenda told him, holding her forehead.

She took a look at her neighbor in his customs outfit.

"Well, don't you look handsome,

Harry?" she exclaimed. "I love a man in uniform. Isn't it considered good luck to bang heads? What are you doing home so early? Is it a holiday nobody told me about?"

"Uh, no," Harry answered her. "I just didn't feel like working the rest of the day, so I excused myself."

Brenda was looking at him flirtatiously. Harry had seen that look before, but he had always had Elaine there to protect him. Now he was miserable and alone until Elaine got home from work at five.

"You know, Harry, you owe me a drink for almost knocking me out. Why don't you come up to my place for a little pick-me-up? I was on my way to the grocery store for a few things, but that can wait. You look a little down. You didn't start drinking without me, did you? Now you definitely have to keep me company while I administer anesthesia to myself. I think walking while intoxicated is a crime of some sort."

Harry felt that familiar ache in his groin. He was surprised he could feel anything besides desperation. He and Brenda were both married to other people. He had always thought of Brenda as flighty and unstable. This was definitely not a good idea. On the other hand, he could use some distraction.

"Sure, Brenda," Harry told her, "but only a quick one. I have things to do." He already had a skin full of Scotch, but it was wearing thin since he had emptied his stomach on the West Side pavement.

They arrived at the Montgomerys' spacious apartment on the fifth floor. Brenda locked the two locks behind them.

*This is not good,* Harry thought when he heard the sound of the locks engaging.

The apartment smelled of air freshener. He saw a green bottle of Air Wick standing open on a side table in the sunken living room. There was a wing-backed sofa and a matching chair covered in a flowery yellow-and-red pattern. There was a maroon leather hassock in front of the chair. Ashtrays sat next to ornate lamps on tables around the room.

Brenda was not a bad interior decorator. A freestanding half-moon bar was in the foyer, with shelves for liquor and glasses on the wall behind it.

"Take off your jacket and stay awhile," Brenda told him, unbuttoning his jacket and helping him out of it. She put it on a hanger in the closet.

Harry undid his collar and loosened his tie. "Okay, but only for a few minutes and a short drink. Then I have to go."

Brenda said suggestively, "Gee, Harry, you look uncomfortable. You know I would never take advantage of you. Our friendship means too much for me to ruin it like that. Try to get those thoughts out of your head, if you can. We're just friends having a drink together. I'm out of Scotch. How about a martini?"

"Yeah, Brenda. A martini would be fine. Please, make it a small one."

"Take it easy, Harry," Brenda said, placing a palm lightly on Harry's chest and giving him a gentle shove. "I won't bite you . . . unless you want me to." She giggled girlishly, turning from him toward the kitchen for ice and olives. He watched her walk away.

Harry was trying not to get aroused. The harder he tried, the worse it got.

When she returned from the kitchen, she removed some of the ice cubes from the bucket and placed them in the martini pitcher around the glass stirring rod. She loved the glazed, scared look in Harry's eyes. She hadn't seen that expression since high school when she would take boys behind the football stadium's grandstand. It excited her to know she was still desirable. She unscrewed the cap from the bottle of gin and poured a liberal amount over the ice in the pitcher, added a splash of vermouth, and stirred.

After she had speared an olive into each of their glasses, Brenda stopped, looked at Harry, and smiled. She didn't want to render him unable to perform. She could see he was frightened but excited. This was no time for talking. The drinks could wait.

She grabbed Harry's tie and pulled him slowly, but firmly, down the hallway toward the bedroom. He resisted, then surrendered, like a difficult pooch.

# CHAPTER 7

## NAKED FACTS

The next morning Brenda exited the elevator in her building's basement wearing a bathrobe over a nightgown. Many homemakers made that early morning trip in similar attire to check on a load of laundry in one of the washing machines. She scooted past the laundry room and out the side door of the building.

She had timed it well. There was Harry about to cross the street on his way to work.

“Harry. Harry,” she called, just loud enough for him to hear.

He turned and walked down the slope.

She loosened her robe to give him a peek at her lingerie.

"I'm coming down to the docks to see you at noon today. Find an excuse to get away for a brief 'conference 'and a private place to have it."

Harry looked terrible, more haggard than at the end of a day at work, and the day had just begun.

"No," Harry retorted, "absolutely not! What we did yesterday was wrong. I refuse to ruin my marriage, or yours either, for that matter, with a repeat performance. We had our little adventure. We are never doing that again. I couldn't sleep last night for the guilt I felt betraying Elaine."

"Just one more time, Harry, please. I promise I'll never ask again. It's been so long since a man handled me the way you did, with that hunger, that force. I've been so bored and miserable taking care of Walter and the kids day in and day out, year after year. Once more, and that'll be all. I know it can't go on, believe me. I wish it could, but I promise it won’t. Don’t make me call Elaine to ask for her permission.”

“Oh, God. Don’t even think about doing that. Okay, okay. Twelve, noon.”

He told her to meet him near the warehouse with his break room in it. “Wear slacks. Nothing too attractive, unless you want to be dragged away by one of the dockworkers.”

That’s all he needed, something else to worry about.

Brenda arrived early, a shopping bag in her hand. She wore slacks, a baseball cap, into which she had stuffed her hair, and a sports jacket that hid her body's contours. Harry made sure to take his lunch hour promptly at noon. He met Brenda and led her into the warehouse. He unlocked the door to his room and hustled her inside. The latch locked itself, but he slipped the bolt home to calm his nerves.

In the shopping bag, Brenda had a

blanket, in case the linen was not up to her standards, which it was not. It was nonexistent.

"I brought a thermos of martinis, glasses, and a couple of peanut butter and jelly sandwiches. I made extras when I put lunch together for the kids. All the ingredients of a healthy diet."

Brenda took the blanket out of her shopping bag and doubled it over on the bare mattress so they would have a top and bottom layer. She took the glasses and put them on the desk. Then she retrieved the thermos and poured them each a drink.

She stripped naked, swallowed her entire drink in a few gulps, and slid under the blanket. Harry obediently followed suit.

When they were finished, he guiltily hopped off the cot and got dressed. He poured them each another drink and handed Brenda hers along with one of the sandwiches from her bag.

Brenda took a sip of her martini and placed it on the floor. “That was nice, Harry. You’re quite good at it, you know. I’ll miss you.”

Harry looked down at Brenda’s figure, outlined by the blanket. She lay seductively propped up on one elbow, her naked arm and shoulder exposed, smooth and inviting, as she bit into the sandwich.

“That’s the way I want it,” Harry told her. “You missing me, this being just a dim memory.”

She had a satisfied grin on her face. It made Harry worry about her keeping her promise not to force him to do this again.

“You’d better understand,” Harry went on, “this is it, for the rest of our lives. We cannot do this ever again, not to your husband and kids, and not to my wife.”

He gave her a worried look. “Besides, I have enough other problems right now to choke a horse. What do you think I was doing home early yesterday when we made our first mistake? Believe me; you do not want to meet the men I'm mixed up with. They are evil people. Consider yourself lucky I didn't ask you to run away with me to the Bahamas. There's no place to hide from these guys. If we did run away together, you wouldn't want to be around when they caught up with me."

He didn't think she was taking him seriously and just gave up trying to warn her off.

"I have to go now," Harry told Brenda. "Take your time getting dressed. The door will lock when you close it on your way out."

He left.

Brenda scampered over to her purse for a cigarette and matches and picked up the ashtray off the desk. She climbed back onto the cot, lit the cigarette, blew out the match, and dropped it into the ashtray. She lay on top of the blanket, naked and exposed to the cool waterfront air, her right calf resting on her bent left knee, basking in the afterglow of a healthy romp in the sack that, she supposed, would have to tide her over for the rest of her life. That was, if she kept her word to Harry. She'd always known Harry Applewood would be good in bed.

Two conspiratorial knocks sounded at the door. *Harry should know by now I'm not modest,* Brenda thought. She tiptoed to the door and whispered, "Who's there?"

A whisper came back, "It's me. Open up. I forgot something."

"Geez, Harry, I'm not shy. You could have just used your key."

Brenda shielded herself with the door, opening it just enough for Harry to slip in.

Evidently, she had not opened it far enough, because the door sprung open and knocked her to the floor.

Brenda looked up at a huge, mean-looking man with a scar down his left cheek.

"Don't be in a rush to put your clothes on, honey. You've got more work to do."

The gorilla closed the door and slid the bolt closed.

Vilma Pelk sat alone at a table in Murphy's Bar on the waterfront. She was actually in her forties but looked to be in her sixties. She had stringy gray hair. She wore rimless dark-lensed glasses, even indoors. In a plain black dress and a black hat like an inverted bowl with a veil folded back over the top, she looked perpetually ready for a funeral. She was one of many eccentric waterfront characters.

"What can I get you?" the obsequious older waiter asked her when he had shuffled over. He covered the breakfast and lunch business at Murphy's before the afternoon crowd streamed in.

It was still morning, but she ordered, "Bourbon, rocks," and placed a Camel in her mouth.

The older man dutifully slid a pack of

matches, with MURPHY'S BAR printed on the cover, from his vest pocket, struck one, and held it under the tip of her cigarette. He shook the match out and gracefully transferred an ashtray from the bar to the table.

"Snack? Hard-boiled egg? A sandwich?" he asked her.

"Yeah. Bring me a baloney sandwich."

The waiter made her drink, then moved away, grateful she hadn't recognized him from the old days in Missouri. He had never met a woman with pure ice water in her veins like Vilma Pelk. She was a piece of work. He'd heard stories that, in her younger days, out west, she'd cut down men and women who stood in her way when she was robbing a bank with a tommy gun, a Thompson submachine gun, without blinking an eye. He had, himself, seen her make a bloody mess with a knife one night, years ago, in a Kansas City speakeasy.

A barely believable rumor had it that Vilma Pelk was actually the infamous Bonnie Parker, who had been caught in a much-publicized ambush with her boyfriend, Clyde Barrow, at Bienville Parish in Louisiana in 1934. Parker was supposed to have died, but nobody who knew Vilma had any question that she could have survived the barrage of machine-gun fire that literally deafened the police for hours after they had emptied their weapons into her and her boyfriend. The waiter didn't really believe that story, but neither did he care to turn his back on her.

He'd quit the mob after the Second World War. Then he moved east to the anonymity of New York City. Evidently, Pelk had done the same.

He pushed through the swinging doors into the kitchen, told the man at the grill to make him a baloney sandwich, and picked up a jar of mustard and a knife to spread it with. After a few minutes, he headed back out with the sandwich, ever the obedient waiter.

When Vilma had finished her lunch, she went out for a stroll. She felt perfectly safe on the waterfront. No one messed with her. She radiated a kind of pain that even husky stevedores steered away from. While she was breathing in the sea air and listening to the water slap against the pilings, she watched the scene with the customs guy and the woman unfold. Vilma had nothing else to do. The woman didn't look like a professional, but, by the way she acted, she wasn't his wife either.

Vilma lit another cigarette and waited patiently.

A while after the couple had entered the warehouse, she saw the customs guy take off alone, fixing his tie as he walked. They must have had a nooner somewhere inside. She spotted the guy with the scar on his face who had been tailing the customs guy. Now Scarface forgot about his man and darted into the warehouse. Vilma knew the woman inside was in trouble. There was nothing for it but to wait. Vilma wasn't about to stop an assault in progress. The woman deserved what she got.

When the dockworker with the scar left to look for his quarry, Vilma went in. She found the door to the room he had left ajar.

"More than you bargained for, eh, honey?" Vilma rasped through her smoke-eroded throat to the tearful, naked woman curled in a heap on the cot. She had a bruise on her face, and her arms were red where they'd been gripped.

"What are you, some bored housewife?"

"That's exactly what I am," Brenda sobbed. "Well, I guess I'm not bored anymore."

"You'd better cover up that bruise on your face and those marks on your arms before your husband sees them," Vilma advised her.

"Are you kidding? He wouldn't notice them if I stood naked in front of him and whistled Dixie. What do you think I'm doing down here, having sex with a married man? I wouldn't even be here if I got some attention at home. Marriage did not turn out to be all I had hoped for."

“I never went the married route,” Vilma commented. She put two Camels in her mouth, lit them, and handed one to Brenda. “I went for the excitement of the open road. Guns, banks, fast cars. I lived hard, almost died hard too a few times. I’m not sorry and, compared to you, I guess I didn’t do so bad. Thanks for the reassurance.”

“You’re welcome, I’m sure.”

“Let’s get you cleaned up, and outta here before the word spreads and someone else decides to have a party with you.”

“God. I’m a mess,” Brenda exclaimed, sucking smoke deep into her lungs. “Just being a bored housewife doesn’t seem like such a bad life anymore.”

# CHAPTER 8

## HARRISON'S PHARMACY

It was a little after seven in the morning. Everyone in Alice's neighborhood was getting up and having coffee, preparing for another day of work.

Manny Harrison looked up from the prescription bench at the back of his drugstore to see one of his customers approaching the door. Manny, the owner and this morning's sole operator, stood on a platform behind his elevated bench wearing a starched white tunic. His black hair was combed over the bald dome of his head, an unlit pipe in his mouth. He was blending an exotic ointment with a spatula on the bench's spotless white Formica surface.

Construction of the apartment building that the pharmacy was in had finished the year before. The tile floors of the store were freshly washed by a professional who made weekly rounds. The merchandise on the gondolas in its center had been dusted by one of the stock boys. The odor of the rubbing alcohol Manny had used to disinfect his bench hung over the premises.

Traffic was beginning to pick up on the street outside.

Lou Morris opened the front door and stepped briskly to the counter for his daily two packs of cigarettes.

"Hiya, Manny. Whatdya know?" he announced. Lou was a perpetually nervous, nattily dressed advertising executive from the building above. He wore his trademark green porkpie hat, which covered a head of prematurely white hair, a bright yellow shirt, and black-and-white-checkered slacks with a white patent leather belt. In essence, it was the classic Miami Beach attire that he loved, totally out of place in the Bronx. His eyes were bloodshot from carousing through the night. Manny had no doubt Lou would still be in bed with last night's date if he hadn't run out of cigarettes.

"Hey, Lou. Whatdya say?" Manny replied, completing their daily ritual.

Manny didn't smoke cigarettes himself; he preferred his more aromatic pipe. Sometimes he even filled the bowl and lit it.

He flashed Lou a friendly smile and put down the spatula.

"I don't say much," Lou answered Manny's rhetorical question, reaching into his pocket to pay for his smokes.

"A pair of dromedaries, if you please."

Camels. Still only in his forties, Lou had the bags under his eyes that burning the candle at both ends produces. He drank, he smoked, he gambled, and he loved to entertain the ladies. He looked like he hadn't had his first cup of coffee yet, but nicotine was his number one priority.

"Thanks, Manny," he told the

pharmacist as they exchanged money for cigarettes.

Lou carefully tore the foil open on one of the packs, dropped the cellophane and foil into the wastebasket next to the register, tapped out a Camel, and lit it with his gold Dunhill.

Without another word, he turned and ambled back to the phone booth in the rear of the store, taking the sports sheet out from under his arm as he went, perusing the nags running to the north at Yonkers Raceway. He sat on the seat in the booth, dropped two nickels into the slot, closed the accordion door, and disappeared in a cloud of smoke. From behind the prescription bench, Manny heard Lou's muffled voice instructing his bookie.

*Crime never sleeps*, Manny thought.

Alice White hurried into the drugstore, the bottom of her nightgown tucked into a pair of slacks and her upper half hidden in a zippered jacket. She walked up to the tall, glass-doored display case that spanned the width of the store, with Manny's prescription bench behind it, and told him, "Good morning, Mr. Harrison. I need toilet paper. I have to quit running out before I notice. Don't stop what you're doing. I can wait."

"So nice to see you, Alice. I don't mind you calling me Mr. Harrison, but most of my customers call me Manny or Doc, whichever you like."

"Okay, Manny, I'll keep that in mind," she responded.

"I hope you don't think it's too nosy of me," he asked her, "but is your friend going to be spending the weekend with you again?"

"I don't mind you asking. Yes, he'll be here Friday night. We alternate between his place in Manhattan and mine. He just finished constructing the sets for *My Fair Lady*, which Julie Andrews is starring in on Broadway. Now he's on call for maintenance. He's going to take our friends from up the Hudson and me to see it in a few weeks."

Manny finished slathering the newly

compounded ointment into a prescription jar and turned on the water to wash his hands. Over his shoulder, he looked inquisitively at Alice. "So, when are you two going to tie the knot?"

"Ugh, Manny, not you too. I'm getting enough of that from my mother and my aunt in Queens. Surely you jest. I've already been married. It was a disaster. At times it was pleasant enough, but in the main, it was a tumultuous disaster. Why would I want to do that again?"

"I just think," he responded, drying his hands and stepping down from behind the bench, "that you two are a perfect couple. I see you arm in arm, laughing, talking, and looking at each other affectionately whenever you walk past the store. Maybe he's 'the One.'"

He retrieved two rolls of Harrison's brand toilet paper from one of the shelves.

Alice didn't mind the harshness of Harrison's toilet paper. Some people joked that it could double as sandpaper, but Manny

Harrison was proud of his retail toiletries line, and, much more importantly, it was dirt cheap.

"Yeah," Alice replied, "he's 'the One ' at this moment, but we don't intend to ruin that by getting married. No offense, Manny, I know you're married, but there's something about getting hitched that makes most people take each other for granted. They do the deed and settle in for the rest of their lives. I'm not saying that's true for everyone, but I see it often enough, and it certainly didn't keep my ex-husband, Andy, and me together. Not even until our first anniversary."

"Does your boyfriend feel the same way?" Manny asked her.

"He feels any way I want him to feel," she said, smiling coquettishly, "at least for now. He's a real gentleman."

"Did the police ever recover that stolen clock from your robbery the other day?" he asked her.

"No, and good riddance to it. I never

could get that thing to work right. The man who does my windows, Frankie the window washer, almost gave me a heart attack showing me how they got in. He jumped from the fire escape through the open bathroom window and landed on the sill. Imagine that, so many stories above the pavement. I almost died. He almost died, as far as I'm concerned."

"Yeah, I know Frankie," Manny commented. "He's quite a guy. I'm not surprised he took that jump. He's got a lot of nerve; shoulda been in the circus."

Elaine Applewood entered the store. The look on her face told Alice she had escalated from mild melancholy to full-blown depression.

"Hi, uh, hello, Alice," Elaine muttered, embarrassed to be confronted by her nosy neighbor at this hour in the morning. She had thought she'd duck in and out of the store without trauma.

"Good morning, Manny," she greeted the pharmacist. "I need some cigarettes, Kents please, one pack, in the box. Then I'll be on my way."

"Okay, Elaine." Alice confronted her. "You have to talk to me now. We can do it here or outside, but I'm right in front of you. I haven't even had my coffee, but you look worse than I feel. Get your cigarettes."

"You have the time, Alice?" Elaine asked her, tears escaping her eyes. "Don't you have to be at work?"

"Yes, but I have a few minutes, and you look like you need a friend. I need coffee, so just let me go next door and get some. Can I get you one?"

"Yes, please. Cream and sugar," Elaine told her.

"You, Manny?" Alice asked.

Manny pressed a key on the register, it opened, and he handed Alice two singles. "On me. Make mine the same as Elaine's."

Alice returned with three cardboard cups of coffee, which she held against each other. She carefully opened her fingers so

Manny could take his and gave one to Elaine, who had lit one of her Kents. Alice popped the top off her coffee and tossed it in the garbage.

"Mind if I listen?" Manny asked Elaine. "If you're going to talk in the store, I'll hear you anyway."

"No, I don't mind," Elaine answered him, "if you really want to. I'm not sure what's going on, and I'm afraid to ask Harry. Thank you both for your concern. You won't tell Harry I talked to you about this, will you?"

"No. I promise," Manny told her. "Just so you know, there's a customer, Lou Morris, in the phone booth in the back talking to his bookie, so keep it down."

Alice declared, "I won't tell Harry we talked about him either, not without your permission. I want you to be able to unload. We're here now, so speak."

Elaine talked just above a whisper. "I can't tell you much, because I don't know much, but it seems to me that Harry's in some trouble at work. He won't tell me about it."

The accordion door of the phone booth squeaked open. Lou walked out of the cloud of smoke to the door.

"Hey, Manny, ladies, nice to see you all," Lou told them, apparently unaware of their conversation. "Have a nice day. I know I will." He smiled, tipped his hat to them all, and left.

"Don't worry about Lou," Manny commented. "The phone booth's almost soundproof, and he was concentrating on the horses."

Elaine paused, wrestled with her loyalty to her husband, then went on. "Lately, Harry's been drinking more than usual, and he's nervous and depressed. He hasn't been sleeping. He tries to put on a happy face, but he's not very good at it. I do hope he's not involved in anything that would endanger his job, Alice. He loves his work."

"I don't know, Elaine," Alice

answered. “Maybe something is threatening him at work. He might just be losing money gambling. Is there a chance he’s having an affair? I don’t mean to be so personal, but you should talk to him, see if he’ll open up. Tell him you’re getting anxious about him. Harry’s a good man. I think he’ll respond to that.”

“Alice, he’s worried about my safety. He asked me to take a leave of absence and get out of town. He’s in serious trouble, and I have no idea how to help him. I feel so alone. I don’t have much nerve when it comes to meddling in Harry’s affairs. He’s got a lot of responsibility, and I don’t want my nagging to add to his worries.”

Manny told her, “I know I said I would keep your troubles to myself, but I have a friend I trust who has connections at the port and may be able to find out what’s happening with Harry. What do you say? Can I run this by him?”

“Harry will kill me if he finds out I talked to anyone about this, but this has been going on long enough. I'm afraid it's affecting his health. Go ahead and speak to your friend, but please be careful. I don't want whatever this is to get worse. I appreciate your help. I really do."

"Don't forget," Alice interjected, "I work for lawyers who can help Harry if he needs legal advice or representation. I hope you don't mind that I've been such a pain in your neck. I can't help myself. It's why I'm becoming a lawyer, so I can get paid to be a pain in people's necks. I'm sorry, Elaine. I didn't mean to pressure you. I spend too many late nights reading Perry Mason when I'm bored with my law books. Maybe there's nothing we can do about Harry's trouble. The least I can do is get you out of town as Harry wants."

"Thank you, Alice," Elaine told her. "I sincerely hope we can come up with a way to give me back my old adorable husband. I'll talk it over with him. He's definitely going to be upset with me, but, at this point, I honestly don't care."

Elaine and Alice left the store together. They finished off their coffee on the street and threw the cups into the trash basket at the corner.

Manny Harrison had returned to his prescription bench and wiped it down with more alcohol. He was now *tick, tick, tick*ing out a label for the jar on his ancient Underwood.

# CHAPTER 9

## DELI WITH THE DAVISES

Milton and Ellen Davis drove down to Manhattan from Stanton, on the Hudson. Alice had become friends with them the previous year. She had traveled to their little town to investigate a murder being blamed on Jim. The Davises were Jim's close friends from the years he lived near them and occasionally worked with Milton. They were amused by Jim and Alice, in awkward alliance. Alice felt guilty about the favor she was about to request, so she asked Jim to get them tickets to *Damn Yankees* and invite them to lunch before the matinee.

"How nice to see you, Alice." Milt rose from his seat in the busy delicatessen. He lumbered around the table and gave Alice a hug and a kiss on the cheek. Milton was a bear, stout, over six feet tall, with bright, watery eyes and burn scars covering the lower half of his face from a boiler explosion in his younger days as a plumber. His big arms were covered with tattoos trailing out from under his short-sleeved shirt. He was in his late forties with a full head of graying hair.

"And I guess it's nice to see you too, James," Milt added with a playful grin. He shook Jim's hand.

Jim circled and kissed Ellen on her cheek.

Ellen reached up, grabbed Jim by the neck, and pulled him down close to her. "We hardly see you anymore since you moved to the big city, young man." She gave him a tight hug.

Ellen Davis was a strong woman with an affable smile. She wore oversized eyeglasses with thick brown frames. She was most at ease in her nursing uniform with a white hat pinned into her hair, but here she was, in a dress, with a handbag, out in public. She wondered how normal women got used to it.

Alice and the two men sat down.

Jim encouraged them, “Everybody order. We don’t want you to be late for your show.”

Milton put on his reading glasses to look at the menu. Though he wanted one, he withheld having a cigarette. The smell of fresh-cut meats of all sorts, fried potato concoctions, chicken soup, sour pickles, and mustard filled the air. The restaurant echoed with the din of a lunchtime crowd. Dishes rattled. Glasses clinked. Big men stood behind the counter in bloodstained aprons carving meat and yelling at the waitstaff, and at customers too.

Milt and Jim had enormous pastrami sandwiches on rye, with potato knishes. Ellen had a corned beef platter with a salad. Alice ordered a hot dog with mustard, sauerkraut, and a pickle on the side. They all had coffee.

"Thank you both for coming to the city today," Alice told the Davises. "My motives for asking you were not entirely unselfish."

"Just spit it out, Alice," Milton told her. "You know us. We'll be glad to help you with whatever you need. Ask."

"Gee, Milton," Alice told him, "and you too, Ellen. You are both such generous friends. I don't mean to be a nuisance. A neighbor of mine in the Bronx, Elaine Applewood is her name, has a serious problem. Her husband, Harry, is in some trouble on the docks at the port. He won't exactly talk about it to her."

Even with the noise, she lowered her voice so the other customers couldn't eavesdrop. "He's with the U.S. Customs Service, and he's been acting funny for a while, depressed, drinking heavily, nervous. His wife asked him about it, and he was very vague, but he did ask her to leave town for a while until he cleared things up, implying she was in some danger. I haven't asked my guys yet, but I think my law firm will agree to let me look into his trouble and see if there's anything we can do for him. Even after I graduate law school and pass the Bar, I think I'm going to keep doing their investigations for them. Jack and Rich have a new associate who does criminal defense work if it comes to that. His name is Clarence Eaton."

"What can we do to help, Alice?" Ellen asked her.

"I called you to see if you would put her up for a little while. We need to get her safely out of town. Then I can begin irritating people, which always happens when I start looking into something like this. She'll pay for her groceries and room. She's a very nice person, but understandably nervous at the moment. What do you say?"

"Oh, Alice." Ellen kept her voice down. "It sounds like another of your terribly exciting cases. I'm sure you would do the same for us if we were in trouble, wouldn't you? Of course you would. Yes, we'll take her in. I can speak for Milton. In fact, I speak for Milton every chance I get, so tell her to keep her money. I have every confidence in you, and I'm sure she does too."

"Ellen, bless you," Alice told her. "You are so optimistic. I don't know how to thank you."

"That won't be a problem, Alice," Milton interjected. "A few more Broadway shows, dinners at fancy restaurants, but I digress. As a practical matter, how are you going to get this woman out of town, up to our place, without attracting attention?"

"I've given it some thought. I don't mean to be overly dramatic. Based on my limited experience as a clandestine operative, I will assume Elaine and Harry are being watched and take measures. Let's do it tomorrow if you don't mind such short notice."

"Alice," Milt told her, "do I have to tell you to be very careful? Once again, you are dealing with invisible forces in a mysterious situation, forces that probably want to hurt these people who are almost certainly withholding information from you. You might as well be blindfolded with your hands tied behind your back. In fact, why don't you shoot yourself in the foot and get it over with? I am apprehensive about your sanity, but, that aside, much more worried about your safety."

"That's kind of you, Milton. I promise I'll take care."

"If you absolutely have to do this, remember," Milt went on, "to look at it like you would a chessboard, from above. People are predictable. Talk to me if you want, and I'll do what I can to help you think along those lines. And please call your gangster friend, Antonio. Maybe this time, he can get involved before anyone tries to kill you."

"Yes, Alice," Jim added. "I would feel much better knowing Antonio was watching over you. He's definitely gonna want to take you to a shooting range to practice with that nice new gun you have hidden in the back of your cupboard. It's in mint condition, never fired, and it's never even been taken out of the box."

“Yes, sir,” Alice responded to Jim. “I will face the inevitable and call Antonio. You’re sure that’s not going to bother you, Jim, him watching over me?”

“Alice, don’t start trying to make me jealous and put you at risk. Besides, Antonio has a woman of his own who looks like she can take care of herself and anyone who messes with him. On top of that, he owes you for fixing the leaks in his security business with those friends of your old office boy, Eddie. You know, Eeny, Meeny, Miny, and Moe?”

Alice groaned. “You’re so close, Jim. It’s Freddie, Tiny, and Pluto, and they’re not a joke. They are as smart as their friend, Eddie, and as streetwise also. Antonio is a gentleman. You can trust him. I’m sorry for giving you a hard time. That’s what I do. You know you love me for it.”

“Yes, Alice, heaven help me, I do. I’m gonna pay the tab and get back to work. They want me to make some changes to the set. That way, it’ll be perfect by the time we all go to see it."

Jim turned to Ellen and Milt. "We're taking you to dinner and *My Fair Lady* in two weeks. Mark it on your calendar. I'll try to get you backstage to meet Rex Harrison."

"What a treat," Ellen replied. "You don't have to do that."

"Yes, they do," Milton put in. "If our guest is still with us, we'll make sure she's comfortable and drive down early."

"Alice, you get back to work now too," Jim told her. "If your bosses end up representing Applewood, convince them to reimburse me for this lunch."

Jim and Alice stood. Jim paid the bill. Alice went around the table and kissed Ellen and Milt goodbye. "I can't thank you enough. Please enjoy the show. I'll call you tonight to set up a time for your guest to arrive. She feels helpless enough, so, please, if she insists on giving you something for the groceries, take her money."

"Okay, Alice," Milton replied.

"Whatever you say. Thank you for the lunch and the show. It's nice having a day off in the middle of the week. See you tomorrow."

Harry fried eggs and made a stack of buttered toast. He laid it all out on the kitchen table. When the coffee was perked, he filled two cups and sat down to eat and read the *Post*.

Elaine came out of the bathroom in a pink terry cloth bathrobe, with a white towel twisted around her hair.

She kissed Harry.

"Morning, honey," she told him. "It smells wonderful in here."

"Good morning, sweetheart," he responded. "You smell wonderful too. Did you have a nice shower?"

She frowned at him. "You look

worried, honey. Don't be. Everything's gonna be fine. My shower was great. Take one after breakfast. It'll make you feel better. I left the shampoo out for you."

"Sounds like a good idea. You want some of the paper?"

"Yes. Give me the movie schedule, please. I don't know how long I'm gonna be gone. Maybe I can put on a mustache and a wig some night and see a picture. I wonder if they even have movies in Stanton."

"Here." He handed her the theater section. "I'm sure Stanton has movies. It's on the Hudson River. Ships stop there on their way up and down from Albany. It's a happening place."

They each read their part of the paper, chomping their eggs and toast, slurping coffee.

Harry asked, "Do you have enough cigarettes?"

"I bought two cartons. They're in the luggage Alice took away last night. That ought to hold me until I get settled, though, frankly, I hope I'm back long before they run out."

"I hope so too."

"Harry, promise me you'll tell Alice everything she needs to know. I don't care. Remember, I love you. We're in this together. Try to accept her help. She has resources, not just legal advice from her firm, but strong men she can count on. I'm only going away so you can stop worrying about me and concentrate on solving your problem."

"I never meant to worry you, Elaine, but I promise I'll do what you say. I'm glad Alice is willing to get involved. I have run out of options."

"Alice has nerve, Harry. I have faith in her. She'll get you out of this mess. Meanwhile, I took five hundred dollars out of our bank account and lined my suitcase with it. That should cover room and board and, maybe, some entertainment."

Harry told her, "I am most grateful to

Alice for getting you out of town, and to you for agreeing to go. Which reminds me, I hate to ask you this, Elaine, at such a time, but what am I supposed to eat while you're gone?"

"Oh, gee, I almost forgot, honey. I made you a bunch of dinners last night and wrapped them in foil. They're in the refrigerator. There are also salad makings that need to be used up. You could throw in a can of tuna fish. If they go bad, dump them in the garbage. The freezer has lamb chops and a steak. I wrote all this down for you and taped recipes to the side of the refrigerator. And you could eat down the hill at Luigi's or across the Concourse at Etta's Diner. Maybe you could eat in Manhattan some night with your coworker. Didn't you tell me a nice young inspector is working with you now? Have a boys 'night out some evening. And, don't forget, the Yankees are playing again, so go to the Stadium some weekend when they're in town."

Harry listened to Elaine, summarizing

his options.

"Nice job," he told her. "Really, thank you for taking such good care of me. I'll miss you, awfully."

He finished his coffee and put his dishes in the sink.

"You convinced me. I'm gonna take a shower."

Harry ran the shower water until it was hot and got in. He hummed nervously as the water poured down on his head. His kidneys had stopped aching, and his urine was free of blood. Maybe things would take a turn for the better, maybe not.

The shower curtain opened, and there stood Elaine. Her bathrobe and turban were gone. She smiled at Harry and stepped in.

"I thought I'd give you something to remember me by, big boy."

Thirty minutes later, they were both dressed. Elaine wore slacks and a blouse. Harry was in his customs uniform. A ship was due in early that Harry was scheduled to inspect. While Elaine straightened his tie, he grabbed her, kissed her, and held her tight.

"Thanks. I promise I will do what you told me to, Elaine, so that you can get back here soon."

"Thanks, Harry. That's all I can ask. I don't want to meddle in your work, but you clearly need help. You look very handsome, my sweetheart. If Alice can arrange it, 'come up and see me sometime,'" she said in her best Mae West imitation.

The day was overcast. It looked like it would rain later. The air was warm. Harry walked down the Concourse to the subway station, a black briefcase hanging from his hand. He stopped at Jimmy's newsstand.

"Morning, Inspector," the newsie greeted him. "Gonna be a busy day on the waterfront?"

"Yeah, Jimmy. A ship's due in I have to look at." Distractedly, he pulled a quarter out of his pocket.

"Give me a *Life*, please."

Jimmy gave Harry a nickel in change. "Life is cheap, ain't it, Mr. A.? You can pull it off the wire. Have a nice day."

Harry responded to Jimmy's joke with a shudder at the alternative meaning, and pulled a *Life* magazine out of its clothespin hanging on the wire.

"Thanks, Jimmy. You have a nice day too."

He took the stairs down into the station.

A short while later, Elaine exited their apartment building and walked to the bus stop. After a short wait, the bus arrived, heading south toward the bustling shopping area on Fordham Road. Alexander's department store and a host of other stores on and around Fordham were popular Bronx destinations. Later in the day, they would be mobbed with shoppers.

At Tremont Avenue, way short of

Fordham, Elaine exited through the rear door. She quickly slid into the back of the station wagon parked just behind the bus stop and got on the floor, pulling the door closed behind her. Alice pulled a blanket over Elaine as Jim pulled away from the curb.

# CHAPTER 10

## PUNISHMENT

Louis Shaughnessy stood in Alfred and Anna Menken's kitchen. Anna glanced at her husband's and his guest's faces, and they both looked away. She placed a cup of black coffee on the table near Louis and left the room.

Shaughnessy was Menken's right-hand man. He was a violent product of the Irish pressure cooker known as Hell's Kitchen, on the West Side of Manhattan. Red-haired, medium height, beefy, and powerful, he was in his late forties.

When his wife had exited the room, Menken folded the paper he was pretending to read and put it on the table next to his glass of milk and plate of cold eggs.

He took a swallow of the milk and grumbled, “Ulcers. Can you believe it? The doc says I gotta lay off the cigars and whiskey and drink this horrible stuff. What do these guys know about anything? Gimme the bottle.”

Shaughnessy took the whiskey out of the cupboard and handed it to his boss, who poured a generous glug into his milk, replaced the cap, and gave it back.

“I don’t like to upset my wife,” Menken lied, pretending he cared. *She can’t wait to wear black at my funeral anyway*, he thought. *Louis can’t wait either. The two of them have been making eyes behind my back for a while now. They must think I’m blind. I’ll deal with that another time. Right now, there’s work to be done.*

Menken asked Louis, “Didja hear about the little ruckus on the docks?”

“Yeah, I heard,” Louis answered. “The

inspector punched the kid in the face, broke his glasses, cut his cheek. The kid has a shiner. It's a beaut."

"That so-called kid deserved it," Menken retorted. "He's been messing with the books, my books. I can't believe he thought I wouldn't notice. He treats me like some idiot. But the customs man is a more immediate situation. It needs attention. You sent Pete and Scar to talk with him like I told you, right?"

"Yeah, of course. They did a first-rate job, without sending him to the hospital, just like you said. The customs guy thought better about ratting out our operation to the feds. He called and canceled his appointment to talk it over with them. They have no idea what it was about. Good thing someone overheard him make the call in the first place. Why?"

"Why? Because I guess he doesn't hear too well. It isn't reassuring. He beat up our man. What disrespect. He's probably shitting his pants now, waiting to see what we're gonna do about it. Maybe he's hoping we'll cut him a break because he changed his mind as we told him to. I bet he's sorry he pulled such a stunt. This might be a good thing, though. He might have accidentally done our job for us, blown off some steam, taught himself a lesson. We have to do him one better, so he never tries this kind of thing again."

Shaughnessy took a sip of coffee and looked respectfully at his boss. He would not want to be in Applewood's shoes. He didn't have to be a genius to know something bad was in store for the customs officer.

Al went on, "I think he's close to cracking up, but I want to give him the benefit of the doubt. Let's say he slipped, didn't think as much as he should have about his pretty wife.

"Just in case, put someone on her, so we know where she is. She's just a last resort. I prefer to hold off on that because it could backfire and we'd have to kill him. He's a war hero, and he wouldn't react too well if we put a gun to her head. He's been doing good for us, just going through a rough patch is all."

"Nice of you to see it that way," Shaughnessy said.

"I just got a great idea," Alfred shot back. "The perfect way to settle him down. It's time to contact our sleeper at customs. This is what I want him to do."

He told Louis.

Shaughnessy could see he was going to be very busy in the next few days.

"Capisce?" his boss asked him.

"*Io capisco*," Shaughnessy replied in Italian, as he had been taught. Then he turned and exited through the kitchen door to the yard. The boss had done good thinking up a way to solve two problems at once and maybe bring Applewood to his senses. Physical pain clearly had not worked.

Menken turned to the racing section of his paper. He took a pull on his "milk" and checked to see who was running at Belmont Park on Long Island.

Alice and Jim were back in the Bronx after a late dinner at the Davises'. Milton and Ellen had graciously welcomed Elaine to their home. Ellen roasted a chicken for dinner. The ladies polished off a bottle of red wine. The men had beer.

Jim was up early the next morning, reading Alice's paper and having a cup of coffee.

The smell energized Alice to finish tying her laces. She came into the small kitchen wearing black basketball sneakers, shorts, and a T-shirt. She smiled hopelessly at Jim, who took his eyes off her legs and looked up at her face. It felt good, but it was so dumb. How had this happened? She had sworn she would never do this again. She bent down and kissed him all over his face. She kept at it until it was time to either to take off her outfit or run.

"I'll be back in an hour," Alice told him

and poured herself half a cup of coffee.

"Good. I'll soak up the paper and take a shower," Jim told her. "When you get back, we can have breakfast. The sky's overcast. You want an umbrella?"

"That's okay," she answered. "The worst happens, I'll get wet. I'm off."

One more peck on Jim's cheek, and she was out the door.

Alice used the solitude to consider what she had stuck her nose into.

She was going to have to sit down with Antonio and get his advice about how to proceed.

Just past Woodlawn Cemetery, she became aware of her surroundings. The businesses on Jerome were closed at this hour on a Sunday morning. She hadn't even glanced at them. There was hardly a car on the road. She had run all the way up the Concourse, up Jerome Avenue under the el, past Mosholu Golf Course, and past

Woodlawn Cemetery, unconscious. Time to turn around and head home. She was ready for a shower and breakfast.

Alice checked in on Harry at his place. They sat at the dining room table, each nursing a cup of coffee.

"Alice, thanks for getting Elaine out of town. She spoke to her boss on the phone yesterday and told him she was called out of state to visit her ailing mother. I think, given the situation, God will forgive her for lying. Her boss told her to take all the time she needed."

"That's a relief," Alice said.

"I'm really not sure you can help me," Harry told her. "These people threatened to hurt Elaine and me both if I don't cooperate. That includes not discussing my problem with anyone, including you."

"Harry, I have people at my disposal who deal with the impossible every day. It would give me great satisfaction to be able to help you and Elaine. I swear, whatever you tell me will remain confidential. If I do have to talk it over with my friends, it will go no further. I take it this is not about a gambling debt or an illicit affair."

Harry cringed. He knew he would have to tell Elaine about what he had done with their neighbor.

"No. My problem at work is not about either of those issues."

"Have you thought about going to the authorities?" she asked him.

"I thought about it. I even made an appointment to talk to the feds, but these people I'm being forced to work for found out and had me beaten up. There was blood in my urine for days. They have connections with the authorities. I'd never live through another attempt like that. I'm passing cargo that I know is not what it says on the manifests. This has gone on for a long time. I have thoroughly incriminated myself. I never thought to hide the money they pay me. I was far too busy worrying about Elaine's and my safety. We've been spending the money like drunken sailors. How on earth can you and your friends help me? I'm going to be caught and sent to prison, not to mention lose my job and leave Elaine destitute."

"Take it easy, Harry. I have no idea how to do this, but I'll think of a way. First, I have to confer with my reporter friend, Franklin Jones, at the *Post*. He probably knows more about Alfred Menken than Menken knows about himself. Then I'll talk to my bosses."

# CHAPTER 11

## AT THE POST

The *New York Post* carried the story. A young man named Irving Teleducci had been shot on the waterfront the previous night. There were no surviving family members. He was an employee of the Dockworkers 'Union. They were paying for his funeral. The police were investigating.

When Harry arrived at work, he heard about the murder. Shame for the beating he had given the young man turned to fear. It was only a matter of time before the police would be around to question him.

He went to his office, shut the door,

and unlocked the desk drawer where he kept his ankle piece. It was gone. Sweat dripped down his forehead. It was crystal clear. He had no doubt Teleducci had been shot with his gun.

He called to tell Alice, then went directly to his warehouse cubbyhole for a drink.

The *New York Post*, founded in 1801 by Alexander Hamilton, was housed in a fourteen-story, Parisian style building between Church Street and Broadway, in the financial district of Manhattan. The paper boasted daily contributions by Drew Pearson, Earl Wilson, and Eric Sevareid. Six days a week, it ran a syndicated column on women's issues by Eleanor Roosevelt, the late president's widow.

After Alice heard from Harry, she

called to make an appointment with her reporter friend, Franklin Jones, for later that morning. Sheltered beneath an umbrella, she headed to the station at 204th Street. Ordinarily, she enjoyed the sound of a torrential downpour bouncing off her umbrella. This morning she was distracted and nervous. Action against Harry had apparently been taken. Death had once again knocked at her door.

She was going up against a person, or persons, willing to use deadly force to get what they wanted. After all her bravado, she was finally scared. She did not care what Antonio told her. She did not have the nerve he credited her with. She was not a killer like he implied she was. She had only done a brave thing last year, saving his and his men's lives during the robbery, because she was stupid and had walked herself into a corner. It was a moment of insanity. That was all. She was really just a victim like everybody else. What was she doing getting into Harry Applewood's business anyway? She must have lost her mind entirely, like Milton Davis had told her she had. Maybe she'd snapped during her marriage to Andy, the cop. Yeah, that was it. Too much time playing games in the bedroom had addled her brain. This was all a terrible mistake. Before she even got on the train, she would call Harry and resign from his case. She had done him no harm. He could take his chances with the police.

After that, what would she do? She could resign from her job at the law firm, quit law school, break up with Jim. That all made sense to her now. Running was her specialty. Who knew? Maybe in her panic, she would become an alcoholic.

Her heart was racing. Her hands were shaking. She hadn't done anything to anyone yet, and already she was thinking about throwing away everything she valued rather than risk hurting people or being hurt. She was getting quicker at becoming hysterical. One bump in the road was all that had happened. True, it involved murder, but she was already dying of fright.

This would not do. She had to pull herself together. And what about Jim? She would marry him and use him as a shield to hide behind, the next thing she knew. What a terrific basis for a relationship. She wondered if that mindset wasn't partly responsible for her failure with Andy, a man who carried a gun for a living. That was not going to happen again. She might as well roll up in a ball and die.

That was entirely enough self-pity, she concluded. Everyone has to die sometime. You might as well stand up straight and have some self-respect. She couldn't believe what she had just put herself through. A doctor would have taken her life's savings for a session like that. She shook it off before she got to the station.

Jones had graciously agreed to meet her with all due haste. She didn't want to waste his time.

"Hi, Jimmy," she shouted, over the noise of the rain, to the newspaper hawker hunched in his shed. "Are you keeping dry under there?"

Jimmy wore a yellow nor'easter so he could pop out to retrieve bundles of newspapers and magazines thrown from passing delivery trucks without getting soaked. It was coming down hard.

"Yeah, Miss White," he shouted back. "The crops musta needed water. You want a crossword?"

"No thanks, Jimmy. I have some thinking to do," Alice replied. "Maybe I'll see you later. I'm going downtown to visit a friend."

She took the D train, standing the first half of the trip, holding on to one of the vertical white poles in the car, barely noticing the world around her. Occasionally she glanced at the ads on the walls, lost in thought about Harry's dilemma. Eventually, a woman near her rose to exit the car, and Alice took her seat. At 59th Street–Columbus Circle, she switched to the C, which took her to Fulton. The whole trip took less than forty-five minutes. She opened her umbrella again and walked the short distance to the *Post*.

Franklin Jones had one in a sea of desks on the tenth floor. An Underwood typewriter was its centerpiece. A large cigarette butt–filled glass ashtray sat beside it. The battle-scarred oak desk looked to be pre–World War I, or maybe pre–Civil War.

Franklin fit right in with the furniture. He was forty-five, disheveled, divorced, the father of a ten-year-old daughter who lived with his ex. He was five ten and rotund, weighing in the high two hundreds. He huffed and puffed over the perennial cigarette in his mouth. He drank heavily, sometimes at work, much more outside the office. His face was flushed from the alcohol and high blood pressure, for which he refused to take the barbaric medicine his doctor had prescribed. So, now he avoided his doctor altogether. Friends at the paper had tried blood pressure medicine and hated it. Better to keel over with a stroke like Franklin Roosevelt had than to live like an invalid on the medicine. “Everything” worked fine, and he wanted to keep it that way. He just had to lighten up on his drinking so he could stay awake long enough to enjoy his much younger girlfriend.

Franklin was a nervous man. No reporter, he thought, ever really got used to the pressure of a deadline, yet he could not live without it. He sat like a sultan on a red velvet cushion atop an oversized swivel chair. He told people the cushion had been stolen from the house of ill repute where he had lost his virginity as a young man. No one believed him, but the story amused them. His tie was askew, his shirtsleeves rolled up. His graying hair looked like he had combed it with his hands. A pair of reading glasses and a pen stuck out of his shirt pocket.

Alice never got used to the mayhem of the newsroom. She spotted Franklin through a cloud of smoke. Cigarettes from every corner of the room contributed to the limited visibility. She wondered how people got anything done with the noise level. It was like Grand Central Station in here, with a symphony of typewriters and loud conversation echoing off the walls. It made the law office where she worked seem like a monastery.

Franklin was deep in thought, clicking away at his typewriter, but he caught sight of Alice weaving a path through the combat zone in his direction. He smiled and waved a burning cigarette at her.

"Nice to see you, Alice," he mouthed.

"You too, Franklin," she mouthed back.

When she was close enough, she spoke audibly, "Thanks for seeing me on such short notice."

"I'm glad you came. I need a break. Let's get out of here. There's a joint a block from here where we can hear ourselves think."

Jones stubbed out his cigarette and rose, pivoting like a ballet dancer to snag the suit jacket off the back of his chair. Alice was impressed with how gracefully a man his size could move.

They took a booth by the front window of Cleary's Irish Pub on Church Street, so they could get what light there was from the cloudy sky. First things first. Franklin downed a shot of whiskey, took a swallow of coffee, lit a cigarette, and, with a flick of his wrist, suavely slid another halfway out of the pack toward Alice.

"No thanks, Franklin," she told him. "I'm trying to quit."

She took a sip from her coffee.

"So, what's on your mind? Just ask." Franklin put his elbows on the table and motioned at the bartender for another shot.

"The docks," Alice announced. "New York Harbor. This morning you reported the shooting death of a young man with the unlikely moniker of Irving Teleducci. I read your piece before I got on the train to come down here. I love your writing, Franklin. Someday, when I'm old and gray, could you write my obituary? What's up with this guy?

Who was he? Who shot him? Why?"

"You know, Alice, you should be a reporter. You ask all the right questions."

He went on. "Irving T. was a child of the docks. An orphan. Got picked up by union boss Alfred Menken through Menken's underlings. Young Irving was smart. Ran messages, carried packages. Even helped with the books. Rumor has it he had a side job selling questionable merchandise around the city and across the river in New Jersey for his boss. Firearms. Some say cheap imitations, smuggled in through the port from Eastern Europe.

"Some weeks before he was shot, a gun dealer from Trenton accosted Irving on the docks, wanting his money back. It seems that quite a few of the guns in his shipment were defective. After a private discussion with two of Menken's large, ugly employees, the dealer decided the guns weren't that bad after all."

"This is good stuff, Franklin."

"Teleducci was shot in the head," the

reporter went on, “twice, at close range. It kind of rules out suicide. It was an execution. One minute he was in Murphy’s Bar on the waterfront having a beer; the next, he was gone. He left a dollar tip, though, under his glass, a gentleman to the end.”

“Hmm.” Alice absorbed the details.

“Who did it?” Franklin asked rhetorically. “Probably Menken’s thugs. You don’t want to mess with those guys or their boss. They are big and very violent. No proof. No weapon. There never is.”

“Interesting,” Alice acknowledged.

“Witnesses saw a U.S. Customs agent beat the victim up sometime during the week before he died,” Franklin told her. “I guess that makes him a suspect too, although, for my money, a weak one. Name’s Applewood. Harold.”

“I know,” Alice told him.

“Why was he killed?” Franklin asked, again rhetorically. “The kid was probably stealing. I don’t know what Menken expected when he took him in. Waterfront 'rats ' survive by stealing. Food. Money. Clothing. So Menken gives him access to more cash than he has ever seen in his life. It's not a big leap to figure out the why of it."

The bartender put some buttered rye toast down on the table in front of the reporter, along with another shot. "You looked hungry," he told his large customer. "It's on me."

"Much obliged." Franklin nodded at the man, handing him the empty shot glass. He tore off a piece of toast.

"Off the record?" Alice asked when the bartender had withdrawn.

"If you say so," he garbled around the toast he had stuffed into his mouth.

"I think the gun they used belongs to that customs inspector you mentioned. He's my neighbor in the Bronx, and his wife's my friend. He's in a bind with Menken's organization. That's probably why he exploded at Teleducci. Still, if the gun turns out to be the one that's now missing from his desk, it doesn't look good for him. The trouble is, we have no proof about any of this. Without the gun, it's a weak case, but if the gun were to turn up, it would have Applewood's prints all over it, and it would certainly, if unjustly, help the district attorney close the matter."

Franklin interjected, "There are two very decent New York City police detectives on this case. They are Andrew Bennett and Scott Gerard. I expect they'll be around to see your customs friend anytime now. They know what they're doing. Still, I would advise him to obtain legal counsel at his earliest convenience, before things get out of hand. I take it you have arranged that with your firm?"

"The attorneys have not yet interviewed Harry, but, as you suggested, I'm sure they will when I ask them to help him. I suppose they'll try to question Al Menken too. And, oh, we have a new criminal defense attorney, Clarence Eaton, who I'm hoping will agree to represent Harry."

"Clarence Eaton, I'm impressed. How did your little firm get hold of such a prestigious attorney? He's legendary. What a coup for your bosses."

"You know they're hungry," Alice answered. "They've always been hungry. They approached Clarence after that murder up the Hudson last year that I helped them resolve. It appealed to him, a legal 'secretary, 'which is probably what he thinks I am, solving a small-town murder. At this stage in his career, he's not really looking for the big bucks anymore. It tickled his fancy like they hoped it would, so he said yes.

"Meanwhile, I'm gonna need my customs neighbor's help to prove his innocence. But it's no good if he's dead."

"No." Franklin raised his brow. "That would certainly defeat your purpose."

"Thank you, Franklin, for helping me. I have to head over and discuss this with Mr. Eaton. I've got an umbrella, so I'll walk you back to the Post."

"No thanks, Alice," he replied. "I don't mind getting wet. I'm just going to sit here and take in this glorious stormy morning before hitting the typewriter again and dashing off another memorable column for the late edition. Don't worry. Mum's the word on your new client, but I'm going to want an exclusive when the job is done. It's gonna make great copy, what with Clarence Eaton for the defense. Okay, pretty lady?"

"Deal."

Jones turned to see the bartender moving his way with yet another shot in hand.

It was still raining pretty hard. Alice opened her umbrella and walked east to Nassau, then north to her office.

# CHAPTER 12

## NYPD

Murphy's Bar was the waterfront hangout for sailors, longshoremen, and the rare civilian who had the nerve to enter it. Frequent brawls over women, money, sports, and card play made the agility to dodge errant punches and flying bottles a necessity. Women, except for the likes of Vilma Pelk, seldom entered the joint unless accompanied by bodyguards. The floor was covered with sawdust to make sweeping up food, broken glass, and blood easier. There was a broom and a long-handled dustpan behind the bar with the shotgun and the baseball bat. The walls were covered with rope, cargo hooks, nets, chains, and other paraphernalia of dock work.

When the place was hopping it was filled with the sound of raised voices and rattling plates. It smelled of garlic, tomatoes, cigarette smoke, and beer. Through the front windows could be seen a daily procession of freighters docked for loading and unloading. The union men who ate and drank here stood in line every morning hoping to be chosen for the backbreaking work. They came to Murphy's to get drunk, blow off steam, and have a plate or two of the owner's spaghetti and meatballs.

This morning Murphy's was quiet. A lone man sat at a table eating scrambled eggs, having a cup of coffee, and reading a newspaper. The old waiter sat on a barstool at the bar drinking coffee and reading a paper himself. Jerry Murphy, the owner, was sweeping up from the night before.

New York City Police Detectives Andrew Bennett and Scott Gerard parked their Dodge and walked two blocks to

Murphy's. Detective Bennett was forty-two years old, five eleven, chunky, and slow-moving. A lit Chesterfield hung from his mouth as he walked. Scott Gerard, ex-army like his partner, was a few years older, an inch shorter, one hundred eighty-five pounds, and well built. His handsome face was still shadowed by the death of his wife several years earlier from cancer. From the way the two men carried themselves, it was clear Gerard was in charge.

Bennett flicked the cigarette off his middle finger into the gutter and pushed through the door into the bar, Gerard on his tail.

Jerry Murphy stood behind the bar in a stained white apron. He had moved to drying glasses and putting them on a shelf in front of the mirrored wall.

"Gentlemen," he exclaimed. "What can I get you?"

*Cops,* he thought.

Even though it was early morning,

Andy Bennett sorely needed a drink, but not in front of his hard-nosed partner. Gerard had made it clear that he did not trust a partner who drank on the job, so Bennett kept it to himself. He put a stick of gum he carried for the purpose into his mouth to cover the smell of the alcohol he had already consumed before coming to work.

Bennett answered, “Coffee.”

“You?” Murphy looked at Gerard.

“Yeah, sure. Black.”

Gerard flashed his badge, though it was obvious the man behind the bar knew what he was.

Gerard announced, “We’re here about the shooting. You on duty last night?”

Murphy put two cups of coffee on the bar. Bennett grabbed his, moved the gum into his cheek, and took a sip. Gerard left his cup where it was.

“Yes, sir,” Murphy replied. “I seen the kid in here having a beer and a cigarette sometime after midnight.”

Bennett asked, “Anything unusual about him?”

“Yeah,” Murphy answered. “He looked more excited than normal, if that’s even possible. He’s always a little squirrely, but last night he was more twitchy than I have ever seen him. He acted like he was waiting for someone. I looked over after a while, and he was gone. His beer was only half-finished. He left a tip under the glass. I didn’t see if he left with anyone.”

Murphy had, of course, seen who had come into the bar and whispered in Teleducci’s ear, then left. The kid’s face had paled and fallen. Soon after, Teleducci slipped the money under his beer and followed the man out the door with his shoulders stooped. Ten minutes later, Jerry Murphy’s keen ears detected two distinct pops. His blood had run cold.

Murphy was not about to risk his neck with that story.

In his office, Harry was having a cigarette. His feet were up on the desk, alcohol coursing through his veins. He and his wife were in enough trouble as it was, and he had compounded it by not only beating up on a man who was later murdered, but by cheating on Elaine with Brenda Montgomery. He would never do anything like that again. He had no idea how, or even if he would ever be able to apologize to Elaine.

A perfect smoke ring floated from his lips as he leaned as far back in his chair as possible. He remembered the sight of Brenda naked with that seductive look on her face.

His drinking at work was getting out of hand. To his thinking, he had already been tried and convicted of the murder of Irving Teleducci. He would fry in the electric chair at Sing Sing like the Rosenbergs. It was cut and dried. There was nothing that the well-meaning Alice White or her friends could do to help him. He might as well sit here and wait for the ax to fall.

*Knock, knock, knock.*

Harry's chair fell over backward, and he crashed to the floor.

"Just a minute," he responded, and picked up the chair, found his burning cigarette, and put it out in the ashtray. Then he got the door.

A military-looking man, medium height, in a gray suit and a matching hat, was waiting on the other side when Harry opened it. Behind him was a similarly clad, heavier version of the same man. Harry had never realized how easy it was to spot police officers in street clothes.

*This is it,* he thought, *the beginning of the end.*

He opened the door wider. "C-come on in."

"Hello, Inspector Applewood. I'm Detective Gerard, and this is my partner, Detective Bennett."

The men put their hats on the coat tree in the corner of the office, and the trimmer of the two showed Harry his badge. He pulled the chair out from the other desk in the office and sat down. His partner stood.

"How do you do?" Harry replied and shook Gerard's hand. He nodded at Bennett.

"We're here to ask you some questions about the young man who was shot last night."

"It was only a matter of time," Harry responded. "I figured you guys would be around about what happened between him and me last week."

"Exactly," Gerard replied. "What did happen? We heard you two had some kind of altercation."

"I wouldn't call it an altercation. It was more like I ambushed a younger, weaker man than myself and hit him twice, the second time after he was down. He didn't have a chance."

"Why?" Gerard asked him.

“The kid was always annoying me, making wisecracks with that horrible Brooklyn accent, asking for money. A few days before I hit him, he yelled a particularly nasty bunch of curse words at me. I was drinking, feeling crappy, looking for someone to take my misery out on, and he happened to be handy.”

“You often drink when you’re working?” Gerard asked, glancing sternly at his partner to bring home what drinking on the job can do to your judgment.

He turned back to Harry. To his trained eye, the inspector already had a skinful at this early hour in the morning. He knew his own partner did as well.

“No.” Harry hesitated. “Well, not usually. Once in a while, I have a shot to break up the tedium, but the day I hit Teleducci, I’m afraid, I had really tied one on. I was sorry afterward, and even more so this morning when I heard he was murdered.”

Gerard asked him, “You’re around here a fair amount, Inspector. Any idea who might have shot poor Irving?"

"No," Harry answered too quickly, "I honestly don't."

"Well, okay." Gerard raised his hands in surrender. "We'll be on our way and let you get back to work. Let me give you my number in case you hear something or remember anything that might be helpful to our investigation."

He handed him a card with his name and telephone number, then shook his hand again. The detectives grabbed their hats.

"We'll be in touch if we have any more questions," Gerard told him. "Meanwhile, have a nice day."

They left.

Harry ran his hands through his hair. He was becoming an accomplished liar. He seriously contemplated having another drink.

"Believe any of that?" Bennett asked Gerard when they were outside. He lit a cigarette to block out the smell of the fresh sea air.

"No," Gerard answered. "It was bull. Something was going on between him and the kid. Even drunk, our inspector is too old and too smart to tee off on someone like that. Then the kid shows up dead. We'll get to the bottom of it."

"Yes, we will."

"If you didn't notice"—Gerard poked his partner in the chest—"Applewood's already been hitting the sauce pretty hard, and it's not even noon."

Bennett shrugged and nodded his head in agreement.

"Let's keep walking," Gerard finished. "That's why they call it legwork."

# CHAPTER 13

## ON THE RANGE

The windows were protected by iron bars. Metal accordion gates guarded the doors at night. The firm's original lawyers, Jack Bryce and Rich Adams, had considered moving uptown, but they were waiting to see how much room they would need to accommodate new members.

Ticking Remingtons, Royals, and Underwoods provided a soothing background for the day's business, especially compared to the newsroom at the *Post*, which was fresh in Alice's memory. Invisible secretaries made their way through the prodigious accumulation of correspondence generated over the past year since Alice had helped the firm successfully represent Jim Peters up north. Publicity in the New York City newspapers had been great for business. Alice's reporter friend at the *Post*, for one, had poured it on.

Jack and Rich met with Alice and their new criminal defense associate, Clarence Eaton, in the conference room.

Laura McDonald, Clarence's longtime secretary, attended the conference and took notes for everyone. She was slim with graying hair, a few years older than Eaton, and wore a charcoal business suit. She was efficient, hardheaded, and, like him, Irish. She managed his schedule, made sure he looked presentable in court, got him coffee, kept him in gin, vermouth, olives, and cigarettes, and bought gifts for clients and, occasionally, for his wife, Janet, and their daughters. In her late forties and widowed, Laura lived with her mother. Not surprisingly, she became good friends with Alice and Edith Burrows, Jack Bryce's secretary. The three had kept select Manhattan bistros open into the wee hours of many a morning, having cocktails and gabbing about everything from fashion to politics, society news, art, travel, romance, food, automobiles, and how wonderful it was to be a single woman living in New York City in the 1950s.

Clarence sat at the head of the table. Notoriously successful in criminal defense, Eaton was intimidating to everybody he encountered except, of course, his secretary, his wife, and his two daughters. They all had him wrapped around their little fingers. His deep and resonant smoker's voice projected well in a courtroom. He was lean, five eleven, with a hard face usually covered with white stubble. However, Laura made sure it was cleanly shaven before he stepped in front of a judge and jury.

This morning he wore the open vest of one of his three-piece pinstripes. His full head of white hair was disheveled. His wire-rim glasses were on his forehead, where he frequently lost them. A pack of Chesterfields sat on the table in front of him, with lighter and ashtray.

Alice filled them in on Harry's situation and his police interview.

Eaton turned to Alice. "I'd be glad to represent Inspector Applewood. I have a friend, a classmate at Fordham Law, named Freddie Quinn. He's a war hero, shot down over Germany a few months before the end of the war. He has a particular interest in labor unions and their leaders. I'll see if he's interested in helping us.

"I read about your excitement up the river last summer, Alice. You did a nice job. I'm going to need you to do more of that same kind of work in this case. At least this time, you know the kind of people you're dealing with going in. I understand you have friends with both brains and brawn."

Alice replied, "One in particular, but he has employees. I need time off with him tomorrow to practice using my gun."

"Excellent," Eaton told her. "Take the whole day. Please, do be careful. I know you're studying law, so I think you'll appreciate the need for extreme delicacy in gathering evidence, especially the methods by which you obtain it. I'll need something to work with in court; therefore, please, call me to discuss your options before you do anything foolish, like breaking the law."

"Coincidentally," Alice responded, "I'm taking Evidence this semester. I'll be careful. I promise I'll check with you if I run into any sticky situations."

"Good. Thanks. I think I'm going to enjoy working with you."

Eaton continued, "You know, Alice, I grew up near the waterfront. A lone woman on the docks is going to attract attention in a dangerous way. Perhaps your friend can arrange some protection for you."

"I don't see how I can avoid that," Alice replied. "I kind of saved him and his men from a bad situation in a garage last year. That's how we met. Now, even if I wanted to,

I couldn't stop him from protecting me."

Jack Bryce spoke up. "Don't be modest, Alice. She saved his life, Clarence. An armed robber had him and his men tied up in a car rental agency and was going to kill them. Alice wandered in to return a car, hit the gunman in the head with a wrench, and knocked him unconscious, almost killed him. Now we get free rental cars forever, and her big friend, Antonio, has become our client."

Antonio Vargas found a space in front of Alice's building. He turned off the engine and rolled down his window. He sat patiently in his Pontiac. The large automobile was one of the few cars that fit his six-foot-two, two-hundred-twenty-pound mass, so he didn't look quite so much like the bull in a circus car he seemed when he drove the cramped rentals he was often forced to use. He wore his trademark black T-shirt, black denim trousers, and motorcycle boots. His only accessory was the diver's watch on his left wrist. His thick dark hair was combed straight back.

It was another beautiful, bright spring day in the Bronx. The Grand Concourse was quiet at this hour of the morning. Nothing but occasional passing buses belching black clouds of diesel exhaust. Antonio was scanning the newspaper one of his men had left in his office. He smiled to himself, thinking about the lovely Alice White. He expected her to keep him waiting. That's why he'd grabbed the paper on the way out of his office. She was hoping he would leave for the range without her. He knew she was not looking forward to training with her gun.

Finally, Alice emerged from the front entrance. She had removed the Browning .380 automatic from the back of the kitchen cabinet and the box of cartridges from the knickknack drawer. They were stuffed in with cosmetics, facial tissues, a roll of nickels, a crossword book, sunglasses, and other assorted female paraphernalia in the oversized handbag she was carrying.

"Thanks for waiting for me, Antonio," Alice told him softly, batting her eyelashes through the open passenger window. "You really didn't have to," she added.

"You are late, as I knew you would be," he replied. "You have had your fun. Now get in the car. This will not be as painful as you think."

Alice got into the car. She thought about kissing Antonio on the cheek but decided against it, under the circumstances. She didn't want to give Jim any more to worry about, and she was sure it would torture him if she displayed any overt sign of affection toward Antonio.

This was going to be serious business. No smoking, no drinking, no joking around. She knew Antonio's rules about firearms. He'd told her exactly how he felt about guns when he first arrived in Stanton last year to help her stay alive while working on Jim's case. An attempt had been made on her life; her brakes were taken out, causing a near-fatal crash into a tree.

Antonio folded the paper and tossed it on the back seat. He started the car and rolled his window halfway up to keep the wind out of his face. Alice left hers down. It was getting hot.

"Did you really think I would leave without you?" Antonio asked her as he pulled away from the curb. "It is going to be a pleasure teaching you to use your gun. I'm taking you to my favorite range."

Forty minutes later, they drove into the graveled parking lot at Coyne Park Gun Range in Yonkers. The lawn between the lot and the office looked recently cut.

Antonio removed a canvas sack from his trunk.

"We're going to be here for a while. Get used to the idea. I brought you lunch. It's in the bag. Sardine sandwiches."

"Thank you."

"I want this gun to be part of your arm," he told her. "I want you to know it and feel it. When you squeeze the trigger, I want you to hit what you aim at. Let us begin."

He spread out a cloth on the bench beside their shooting position near the middle of the wide outdoor range behind the office.

"You need to break the gun down, clean it, oil it, and put it back together. You're going to do that over and over until you can do it blindfolded."

He walked her through the process and had her repeat it four times. When she was done, the gun was clean, the slide was smooth, and she felt a degree of ownership and fondness for the weapon she had not anticipated.

"You'll do it some more before we leave," he told her.

He demonstrated how to press bullets into a magazine, snap the magazine in place in the handle, and slide a cartridge from it into the chamber. He insisted she not point the gun at any part of herself or anyone else, loaded or unloaded. He told her that once, a man standing next to him at this very range had shot himself through the heart with what he thought was an empty .45. She was to keep her finger outside the trigger guard unless she intended to fire. He reminded her about the safety; forward off, backward on. He told her to carry a spare magazine on her person, in a pocket, not in her purse—the same for the loaded automatic itself. Otherwise, if her purse got away from her, she would be out of luck. She might want to get a clip-on holster, but in the meantime, tucking it into the waist of her slacks, or her belt if she were wearing one, would do.

After she demonstrated proficiency in seating and ejecting the magazine, sliding one in and out of the chamber, safety on, safety off, he told her she was ready to fire the weapon.

"I brought earplugs for us both, but I want you to shoot a few rounds without them, so you know what it will sound like when you do it for real. At this distance, do not aim for the head. Shoot for the center of the chest. If you are close, you can use the head. Remember, when you shoot, shoot to kill the person you are aiming at, not to wound them.

Get that straight right now."

Alice frowned. "You see, Antonio, with all due respect, that is something I'm having trouble with. I'm getting queasy just thinking about it. That's why it took me so long to get up here with you."

"I understand, Alice. It is a good thing, not a bad thing that you hesitate to kill someone. But this is the life you have chosen, or the life that has chosen you. Either way, you have no choice. It would help if you accepted that you were meant to do this thing, to either kill or die. It may never happen, but, if it does, make no mistake, you must stand up and take care of the business in front of you."

"Why, Antonio? I don't think I have this in me."

"It does not mean you are not a good person or that the person you have to kill is not good. It means that you must trust your judgment as much as I do. Believe me, after the robbery last year, I would trust you with my life. When you decide to kill, that is the end of deciding. It is done. Right then and there, you must clear your mind of all doubt. It would help if you did that right now also, here on this range. Using a gun is about protecting your life. It is about your survival and the survival of people you value who are counting on you. It is not meant to scare anyone, especially not you. It is meant to stop someone from killing you. You can only do that by ending their life. It is not enough to merely wound them, because wounded people can pull a trigger, and you are dead."

He raised his voice and intention. "DO YOU UNDERSTAND?" He looked directly into Alice's eyes with that piercing glare she could not resist. "Get it straight."

Fear rose from Alice's stomach. She did not feel physically threatened by Antonio. On the contrary, she could tell he honestly feared for her life and wanted her to do the same.

For once, Alice was speechless. The witty banter failed her. She became calm. She felt serenity descend on her. She took a deep breath. Her body relaxed. Something had happened to her while Antonio was speaking. Something had seriously shifted. In the silence, the responsibility for life and death had magically transferred from him to her, and a door had closed behind her. There was no going back. She could never pretend to be a victim again.

She stared into Antonio's eyes, his gaze piercing, and felt the dampness of animal excitement cover her. It wasn't just physical attraction, although, didn't she know, even at this major, cataclysmic turning point in her life, her reproductive nature found it necessary to assert itself. Yet, she admitted to herself, it was more than that. It was a different kind of bonding, a recognition of their common nature. Beauty, if she said so herself, had been infected by the Beast. Of course, she would never call him that to his face. For better or worse, she was capable of being as much of a cold-blooded killer as she knew he was. It didn't feel terrific, but neither did it feel as bad as she had feared it would if she ever allowed it to happen. It just felt like the way it was.

It had taken her all this time, all these years of being alive, to get it straight, who she was. Last year she had struck a man in the head with a wrench, hard enough to crush his skull and kill him, to protect innocent people, relative strangers. If he had died, she knew, it would have had to have been okay. She was excited when she did it, even terrified, but she knew what she was doing. She did it in cold blood. She knew she might kill the man, but she did it anyway. She had no choice. She would do it again if the circumstance dictated. Even after she did it, she had not appreciated how much it had redefined who she was and what she was capable of.

Alice's whole body hummed, her breathing stilled, her blood cooled, her vision sharpened. She smelled the recently cut grass for the first time since getting out of the car. She heard the traffic going by on the highway nearby. A bird was chirping. She took another deep breath and let it out.

"Okay," she announced. "I *do*

understand. For the first time in my life, I think I understand. Thank you, Antonio, for bringing me here, even against my will. After last year's trauma, you'd think I would have gotten the message, but I still did not understand. You tried to tell me, I remember, but I didn't hear you. You asked me to work for you as a bodyguard. I thought you were flattering me. I didn't want to think I was that kind of person, capable of using charm to move in for the kill like you told me I could. I preferred to think of myself as a victim, a scared, defenseless female. How amazing that you had the patience to wait me out until I saw the truth. I am a horrible person, aren't I?"

Antonio looked straight through her. He smiled just a little. It was deliberately flirtatious and had its intended effect. Though, with that feeling in the pit of her stomach, she also felt an expression of brotherly love. She was almost forty, for heaven's sake, an old lady, way too old to be having this happen to her. She was in love with two men. She would have to put this aside until . . . until forever.

She snapped out of it, focused on his eyes, and heard him say, “Horrible? Yes, maybe, but now you are a formidable enemy, Alice White, and you are also a powerful friend.”

The target was a black cameo of a head and torso without arms or legs. It hung from a rope strung like a clothesline on pulleys, near to far, so its distance could be adjusted.

“We’ll start at ten yards until you get used to the sound and hitting the target where you want to hit it. You have to imagine it shooting back at you, so you feel the fear you will when the time comes. Don’t worry about how you will deal with it afterward. If you live to regret it, you will find a way to handle that.”

“Geez, Antonio. I’m shaking, and I’m not even in any real danger.”

“Wrong! You are in real danger, Alice, right now. These people have killed someone. They shot him twice in the head. He was unarmed. Everyone shakes when they shoot at someone. That does not mean they don't hit what they aim at. And people don't stand still when you shoot at them like that target. You have to move your body to keep up with them."

"Okay."

"I have seen you in danger," he went on. "You knocked that junkie out cold in the garage. He had a gun and was going to kill you, me, my men, and Pete, the owner. Remember the feeling? You were scared, but you did what you had to. I'll bet you didn't stop shaking for a whole day afterward. Alcohol didn't help either, did it? So what? You did that, and you can do this. And you're going to come up here to practice with me again, so if we get caught flat-footed, I know I can count on you. Even when you become a lawyer, you're going to be happy you know how to use a gun. Who knows, you might even get to like it."

"Okay, Antonio," Alice said. "Put in your earplugs and stand back."

# CHAPTER 14

## JOTARO SARISOTO

"Is he in?"

Laura McDonald looked up. "Yes, he's here, Alice. Is this about Applewood?"

"It is."

"Just a minute," Laura told her. "I'll let him know you're here."

Laura didn't use the intercom. She knocked once and entered Eaton's inner sanctum without waiting for a reply. If she was going to interrupt him, she needed to take down his instructions for her on the case laid out in front of him.

"Sorry to disturb you, boss. Alice

White is here about Applewood."

Eaton broke his intense preoccupation with the papers on his desk and looked up.

He slid his glasses onto his forehead.

"Yes, okay. That's fine, but first, this motion"—he handed her a stack of papers—"needs to be typed and filed with the court."

"Got it."

"Also, please call my wife and tell her I promise to be home in time to take her to Mayor Wagner, Jr.'s reception and to please have a cocktail waiting for me so I can start drinking while I'm dressing."

Mayor Robert Wagner had died two years earlier, and his son had won the election to replace him.

"Right," Laura responded. "You only have thirty minutes until your next appointment."

"Then let's make the most of them. Show Miss White in."

Alice sat in the client chair. Eaton lit a Chesterfield, then motioned to the pack, indicating she could smoke one if she liked. It was still early in the day, and already two people had tampered with her resolve not to smoke.

"No thanks, Mr. Eaton. I'm trying to quit."

"Fair enough. Please, Alice, feel free, when there are no clients present, to call me by my first name. How did it go on the shooting range with your friend?"

"Incredibly well, Clarence. Better than I thought it would. He worked me over, breaking my automatic down and putting it back together, shooting with and without earplugs. It was an experience I will never forget."

"Good. I'm happy you did that."

"He'll be taking me back there. He warned me that we are not through."

"Excellent, Alice. Now tell me what is happening with the Applewoods?"

"Mrs. Applewood is still safely stored away out of town with friends of mine. The two New York City police detectives assigned to the Teleducci murder have not returned to question Harry again. If I didn't tell you already, their names are Scott Gerard and Andrew Bennett. My friend at the *Post*, Franklin Jones, says they're good at what they do. Harry thinks they'll want to question him again because he lied, and he believes they knew it. There were witnesses to his assault on the victim the week before the shooting. He said he was drunk, but he left out the real reason for his anger."

Alice went on, "Harry believes that the young fellow was probably killed with the .38 Special he keeps in his locked desk drawer. It's gone. Franklin told me there's a rumor that Teleducci dealt cheap Eastern European copies of American firearms for his boss, Alfred Menken. The kid also kept his books. He thinks he was probably skimming union funds. Killing him with Harry's gun addressed two problems for them. There's no proof of any of this. To get it, I would have to infiltrate the waterfront and customs somehow. Risky business at best."

"Yes, Alice, extremely dangerous."

"It seems to me, however, that the person best suited to help us get proof is Applewood himself. All we have to do is keep his wife safely out of the way. What do you think, Clarence?"

"What you suggest makes sense to me, Alice, but, just as I said about you, I'd like to give him as much protection as possible too. I don't think Inspector Applewood should invoke his right to an attorney unless they challenge his story about the assault. After all, he's innocent, at least of the murder. Need I say, Alice," Eaton concluded, "that I want you and Inspector Applewood to be very careful. There's going to be many more cases I will want you to help me with, so stay alive and make sure our client does the same, please."

"I'm on it, Clarence."

Japanese martial arts developed in the tradition of the warrior class, the samurai.

Jotaro Sarisoto was trained in Bushido, the warrior's way, by his father's older brother, Hiroki.

At the age of five, Jotaro was sent to live with Uncle Hiroki for seven years.

"We are here in the snow of this mountain pass to begin your training. You are embarking on a serious journey, Jotaro," his uncle told him. "The cold is your first lesson. You will train to overcome fear, pain, and fatigue. Never forget that I love you, and never forget the warriors that came before us."

Hiroki prepared tea for them on the small fire he had built.

After serving his nephew, he began. "I want to recount for you the life of Miyamoto

Musashi, the Blade Master, the greatest warrior of all time."

Hiroki talked on until sunset. Jotaro was forced by circumstance to play his attention between the heat of the fire and the fascinating odyssey of the swordsman who was to become his lifelong inspiration. Hiroki impressed his nephew with the physical discipline of fighting and its spiritual and moral dimensions.

"Tomorrow, we will return to this spot. I will meditate while you stand on one foot. After lunch, I will resume my meditation, and you will experience the luxury of standing on the other foot. I am proud that you have adjusted to the cold so readily. That will serve you well in combat."

In his early years of training, Jotaro would often fall on the hard ground from exposure and exhaustion. As he got older, the falls disappeared. His jumps became graceful leaps. His crash landings assumed the delicate grace of a bird returning from flight. He came to move along the ground with the agility of a deer.

He learned to use the knife, the shuriken, the razor-sharp throwing star, the sword, the chain, the bow and arrow. He grew into a behemoth. Unlike his sumo counterparts, he was solid muscle, very little fat. He worked with bokken, wooden swords, two at a time. When he twirled them, he appeared as if a windmill in the gale.

When he went to war for Emperor Hirohito in the 1930s, firearms were added to his armamentarium.

As a soldier, Jotaro distinguished himself through bravery in battle.

However, there was a dark side to Japanese military service that forever damaged the warrior's soul. It was the torture of Allied prisoners. It appalled and depressed him. It betrayed the spiritual values he was trained to live by.

Deeply troubled when he was released from military service, Jotaro emigrated to the United States. Plagued by guilt and shame, he set out to do penance for the crimes he had committed, many of which were against American prisoners. He settled into Hell's Kitchen and the Port of New York, where he found work as a longshoreman. As expected, his nationality provoked many violent confrontations. Fellow dockworkers had lost family and friends in the Pacific. Some had themselves survived capture and imprisonment by the Japanese under the most horrific conditions. In the early years after the war, Jotaro often asked himself why he had not simply taken his own life rather than participate in those atrocities. It would have been the honorable thing to do. Instead, he had taken the coward's way out, and now, he badly needed to pay for it.

He restrained his martial capabilities and deliberately submitted to beatings of atonement.

Only once did Jotaro lose his temper. That had resulted in a prison term. Convicted and sentenced for aggravated assault, self-defense was hardly an acceptable excuse for a former Japanese soldier living in America in the 1940s.

During his time in prison, Jotaro met Antonio Vargas. Antonio was another alien to the United States, serving a powerful man's prison term in exchange for the man’s favor.

“Jotaro,” Antonio told him. “you are as fine a person as I have ever known. What you did in the war has not taken that away from you. There is a reason we have met here behind bars. We are both learning to forgive ourselves and, maybe, other people, and to move on with our lives. Just as the death of Jesus Christ forgave Christians their sins, we must forgive ourselves for the harm we have done others. Forgiveness is what we have to offer each other, Jotaro. Please teach me to meditate and to fight, like you do, with less force and more effect than I have now. If there is a God of warriors, which we both believe there is, we have paid him sufficiently for our disgraceful behavior.”

After being released from prison, Jotaro

returned to dock work, and Antonio was set up in the security empire he had earned by serving his prison term. He would provide security for a significant portion of Manhattan's restaurant and entertainment industries.

By 1956, Jotaro had settled into a tense peace with his fellow dockworkers. At six foot six and two hundred and forty pounds of solid muscle, he did more than his share of the heavy lifting on the docks and, despite his nationality, had gained some measure of respect.

His colorful shoulder tattoos had been embellished in prison. He kept his shiny black hair clean and tied back in a ponytail. He wasn't exactly friendly, but he no longer growled audibly at his fellows to keep them at bay.

Antonio loved Jotaro like a brother, trusted him, knew Jotaro was a man of his word.

“Jo?” Vargas rang and caught Sarisoto in. “Long time. We need to talk.”

“Anything you need, Antonio-san,” Jotaro told him. “I’ll be there. Where and when?”

“Now. The steak house on Williams. It is closed. Go around back.”

Delmonico’s on Williams Street in Manhattan was closed to the public before noon. After an impressive hug, the two huge men sat down in an otherwise empty restaurant. Theirs was the only table covered with a white linen cloth.

The place had just been mopped down. Inverted chairs rested on bare tables around them. They could hear workers' sounds from the kitchen, performing their daily chores, and conversing in English and Spanish.

Mario, the manager himself, in an open-collared white shirt with the sleeves rolled up, brought them two cups and a pot of coffee on a tray.

"Anything else for you and your friend, Antonio?" he asked. "Can I cut you each a nice steak sandwich? Delmonico, of course."

"How about it?" Antonio asked his friend.

Jo smiled. He loved steak. Now, they were sitting together in this fancy steakhouse his friend provided security for.

"Sure," Jo answered. "I would appreciate that very much."

Mario nodded and disappeared into the kitchen.

"What's happening, Antonio?" Jotaro asked his friend.

"I need your help," Antonio answered. "A year ago, this junkie got the drop on me and a few of my men in a rental garage on West End Avenue. We do their security and move cars around the city for the owner on Fridays. For a strung-out guy," Vargas continued, "he was smart enough to have them tie me up first so I wouldn't accidentally break his neck. They slipped me a wrench while they did it. When he got everyone tied up, he started waving his gun around like he would kill us all after he got the money he needed for dope. In walks this nervy, good-looking woman returning her car, Alice White. She sits down next to me on the floor, slips me her pocketknife to cut myself loose, and takes the wrench out of my hand. Then she stands up and gets close enough to this crazy guy to hit him in the head, hard, and put him down. It was awe-inspiring. Now, I owe her for the rest of my life."

"Yes, I see."

"She's got this customs-inspector neighbor. He lives in her building in the Bronx, works here, on the docks. The union boss, Menken, has him by his private parts, forcing him to turn his back on guns coming in through the port. Menken's guys threatened to do bad things to his wife and him, then kill them both. The inspector's been showing signs of wear—beat up the bookkeeper, one of Menken's employees, who's been stealing from Menken. They stole the customs guy's gun from his desk and executed the bookkeeper with it to straighten them both out."

"Yeah," Jo spoke. "I bet I know the guy they killed. Skinny college kid. He's been hanging around the docks since he was little, graduated to doing their books. They trusted him. Stupid. He got caught with his hand in the till, and they executed him."

Antonio told Jotaro, "Alice White, she moved this customs guy's wife out of town and hid her away someplace safe. Now she wants to snoop around the docks and get proof that Menken set him up. A pretty woman alone on the docks won't last very long without protection. That's what I want you to do for me. And she's gonna need some help watching the customs man too."

"Yes," Jotaro replied without hesitation. "I'll do it."

"Follow her. Don't let her get hurt, okay?"

"Sure, Antonio. Anything for you. I'll

keep an eye on her and her friend. If I need another guy, I'll let you know."

"Right, exactly. Thanks, man. You'll like her," Vargas told him. "She's a lady, but she's got guts."

The steak sandwiches arrived, along with two salads and two glasses of beer.

The men thanked Mario and clinked glasses.

"Stay in touch, Jotaro-san," Antonio told his friend.

# CHAPTER 15

## JACKSON'S STEAKHOUSE AND OYSTER BAR

Harry had stopped at a deli for coffee and a roll on his walk from the train to work. These he placed on his desk. He was not sleeping well without Elaine. Gin and cigarettes did not help. It was his third cup of coffee this morning. His eyes burned. He would have to make sure he assigned himself the Spanish freighter for inspection.

"Hey, Phil." Harry sat at his desk and greeted his uniformed colleague when the young man arrived, late as usual.

"Hey, Harry. How're you doing? Did ya have a nice weekend?" Phil asked him.

Philip Madison was twenty-six. He owned two specially tailored customs uniforms, one of which he wore now. His sandy hair was neatly coiffed, his uniform pressed, and he was ready for action. He looked like a poster boy for the United States Customs Service. *Become a U.S. Customs officer and live the life of a Hollywood star*. He was a smooth-talking, martini-drinking ladies 'man, what they called a "hail-fellow-well-met."

"Fine," Harry answered. "Elaine went off to Minnesota to see her parents. I've had a devil of a time sleeping without her."

Phil tapped out a Winston and lit it with his Zippo. Like everything else Philip owned that had room for it, the Zippo was elaborately embossed with the U.S. Customs seal, an eagle with a stars-and-stripes shield across its chest, "Vigilance, Service, and Integrity" in a circular border with the year 1789 at its six o'clock.

He exhaled smoke. “If your wife is out of town, how’s about we go out for drinks and dinner after work?”

“Funny you should ask, Phil. Elaine suggested that very thing before she left. She put all sorts of dinners in the refrigerator and left written instructions for preparing them, but I’m not much of a cook. That’d be great.”

“Okay then, what’s on the schedule for today, Harry?”

“Two freighters. The *Prince Willie* out of London and the *Caldra* from Valencia. If you don’t mind, I’ll take the *Caldra*. I feel like practicing my Spanish.”

“Fine with me, Harry. You’re the boss. Just stay away from that raw Spanish food. I don’t want you getting sick on me. Stick with a cup of coffee if they offer you something to eat.”

Applewood just wanted to get started. He was on edge and needed something to do. The *Caldra* had a large shipment of “olive oil” aboard he needed to look out for.

Harry was feeling a twinge of optimism. It might not be warranted, but at least he was no longer alone. He and Elaine might still be killed. Prison time was a distinct possibility in his future. He might be convicted of the murder of Teleducci or sent to prison for betraying the trust of the federal government, or both. But anything was preferable to continuing the way things were.

His career was definitely over. If he survived, what would he do for a living? Fortunately, he and Elaine did not have any children. He would have gone crazy if they did, and his kids were being threatened to keep him in line.

He missed Elaine. What was he going to do without her to keep him warm at night until this was over? Their man-crazed neighbor, Brenda Montgomery, had better stay away from him.

Philip Madison had grown up in the historic town of Groton, Connecticut, near the naval base. Navy kids came and went from his public school. They treated the townies like trash. Madison's sister had been taken advantage of by more navy brats than he could count. Much to his hardworking parents' dismay, Philip was forever getting into fights with the privileged children of navy personnel. It was a dog-eat-dog childhood, and Phil's family could not begin to understand what he was up against.

He may have despised the navy, but he loved the sea—the smell, the taste, and the beauty.

He was too young to serve in World War II. When he was old enough, he sought employment with the United States Customs Service, requesting assignment to seaport installations. The Coast Guard sounded like too much work. Customs was a perfect fit. He got to wear a sharp-looking uniform and gain a measure of the respect the navy kids 'fathers had gotten when he was growing up. He worked on the waterfront, first in New Haven, Connecticut, then on the more prestigious docks of the Port of New York and New Jersey.

His family was thrilled when young Philip moved to New York City and began work at its port. To them, it meant he was moving up in the world. His uncle already lived in New York and did some work connected to the waterfront. He wouldn't be completely alone.

Jackson's Steakhouse and Oyster Bar, at Pearl and Whitehall Streets, was not far from the port facility. Harry liked it because it was more elegant than most of the bars and restaurants near the docks. There were white cloths on the tables, and the floor was not covered with sawdust. The men wore suits and the women dresses. There was a little vase with flowers on every table and a lit candle.

It had a dark blue awning with JACKSON'S STEAKHOUSE AND OYSTER BAR written on it, extending from the entrance to the curb. A doorman opened and closed the front door and ran out to let customers out of automobiles and limousines. He also escorted older clientele across the sidewalk.

Harry arrived in his uniform and asked for a booth in the back. He checked his hat with the girl managing the coatroom, a very pretty young woman, on his way to the table. The danger he was in was making him entirely too hungry for female companionship. She was clearly young enough to be his daughter. He wished his wife was there. Thank goodness there had not been any word from Brenda Montgomery since their afternoon tryst on the docks. He was not sure he could have resisted her at this moment. Maybe she would keep her word and stay away from him. He had to arrange to sneak up to Stanton and spend some time with Elaine.

The waiter, older than Harry, probably in his late fifties, wore a black bow tie and vest, with a white apron from waist to knees.

Harry looked at him and wondered, ironically, if he would even be able to get a job like that after he was released from prison. The waiter placed a clean glass ashtray and book of Jackson's matches on the table and went to fetch Harry's martini: dry, straight up, with an olive. Harry lit a cigarette.

Phil Madison slid into the booth opposite him.

"Hello, Harry. How'd it go today?"

"Fine," Harry told him. "I got by with my broken Spanish, and I didn't let them feed me a thing, though they tried. How'd you do with the Brits?"

"Everything was ducky, Harry. Tea and crumpets on the bridge after the cargo was inspected. The crew was nice enough—a successful day for United States Customs.

"Another one of those if you would," Phil told the waiter when he arrived with Harry's drink.

Phil lit up and placed his ornate lighter on the table.

"Did you get a load of the girl at the coat check?" he asked Harry.

"Yeah, I noticed. Quite a beauty," Harry answered. "But too young for me."

"I made a date with her after she gets off tonight. I love wearing my uniform out to dinner. Want me to see if she has a girlfriend? You must be lonely without your wife."

"That's okay. I'm saving myself for her return. But thanks anyway."

Philip Madison knew all about the woman Harry had met on the docks and taken into the secret warehouse room he kept for rest and recreation, but he didn't want to embarrass his fellow inspector and ruin a good dinner. He was starved.

Phil asked him, "Is Elaine getting home before this weekend? Maybe we could catch a game at the Stadium."

Harry wanted to spill his guts. He had been alone and afraid for so long. Now he had allies. They were promising to end the nightmare he and Elaine had been living. It was making him downright giddy. But Harry was still on his guard. He knew they were in more danger than ever.

Instead of telling his coworker everything, he replied, “Gosh, Phil, you and Elaine must have talked about me before she left. Besides having dinner with you, she encouraged me to see a game when the Yankees were in town. If you’re up for it, I am.”

“Sure. That’d be great. Where does Elaine’s family live?”

“I told you before. Elaine’s parents live in Minnesota.” Harry wondered whether his colleague just had a bad memory or was checking to see if he was telling him the truth. He went on, maintaining the charade. “When she’s coming back depends on how her mother is doing. Her mom’s been sick, and her father hasn’t been coping very well. I told Elaine not to rush home, but I think that was a mistake. I’m missing her more than I thought I would, and she only just left.”

The waiter brought Philip’s martini,

and the men sat back, relaxed, and had their drinks and cigarettes.

They ordered a dozen oysters on the half shell. Philip squeezed a lemon over them and a splash of Tabasco. They dug in, dipping them in Jackson's signature sauce.

"Man. This is the way to finish a day inspecting ships," Philip exclaimed, lifting the martini to his lips.

They had steaks for dinner—medium rare—asparagus, and baked potatoes.

During brandy and cigars, they discussed the Yankees 'chances at another pennant.

"This was great, Harry," Phil told his colleague. "We have to do it again, maybe make it a regular thing."

"Yeah, Phil. I needed to relax. Thanks for asking me to join you."

"I'm going to hang out at the bar and wait for my date to finish work," Madison told him. "See you tomorrow."

Harry stopped to collect his cap. He

tipped the adorable girl at the window of the coatroom, envying Phil his date with her.

It was raining. He raised his collar and strolled toward the subway station to catch his train north. The wet felt good. He turned his face up into it.

Phil went to the pay phone on the wall next to the bar at the front of Jackson's. He dropped in a dime and dialed. After a pause, he spoke, "His wife's out of town. She's visiting her sick mother in Minnesota."

The large Japanese man slid off a barstool, leaving a dollar bill next to the remains of his beer. He headed out into the night to catch his charge before he got to the train station.

# CHAPTER 16

## CONJUGAL VISIT

Harry Applewood awoke after another restless night. He flipped through yesterday's late edition of the *New York Post*. It had been sandwiched between the doorknob and the jamb last night when he returned from dinner. The coffee finished perking, and his toast popped up. The box he was locked into seemed to have shrunk with the Japanese bodyguard's revelation that his seemingly innocuous fellow customs officer, Madison, was in league with the enemy. Alice White's friend, Jotaro, had caught up with him at the station and made sure he got safely home. Now he knew Phil Madison was not his friend, and he was grateful he had not told Phil where Elaine really was.

His physical yearning for her seemed to have perversely increased in proportion to the amount of trouble they were in. He would not make it to the weekend. He was forty-eight, entirely too old to be feeling this way about a woman, or women in general, he thought. That utterly inappropriate romp with their neighbor had completely upset his hormonal balance. As far as his marriage was concerned, it had been a horrible mistake. Still, it had, in effect, increased his passion for his wife. That was not an excuse for his behavior. Brenda Montgomery had not forced him into bed. In giving in to his baser instincts, he had displayed the emotional maturity of a teenager. Elaine deserved better. Someday he would have to come clean with her. He wasn't sure he could do it, but he knew he must. He prayed she would forgive him when he did.

Meanwhile, he needed a plan to see Elaine; the sooner, the better.

He picked up the phone and rotated the dial.

"Hello," Alice's groggy voice answered.

"Hi, Alice. I'm sorry if I woke you. It's Harry."

"Yeah, Harry. You did me a favor. I fell back asleep after the alarm went off. Now I have time to get cleaned up and have breakfast before I head downtown. You sound a little tense. What can I do for you?"

"I won't keep you on the phone, Alice. Thank you very much for your friend Jotaro's protection and counsel. If he hasn't already told you, my coworker, Phil Madison, is an agent of the bad guys. Jotaro overheard him reporting in on where I told him Elaine was. Thank God I didn't tell him the truth like I was tempted to. I am so relieved to have you and your friends on my side. I have to watch what I say. I told Phil that Elaine was in Minnesota with her parents. How stupid could I be? It was just the first place that came to mind. Maybe I should have kept my mouth shut altogether."

"No harm was done, Harry, just as long as you stick to that story."

"It's embarrassing at a time like this, but I need to see Elaine very much. I'm going to go crazy if I don't spend some time with her soon. I don't want to be a pain in the neck. I know you only just drove her out of town. You've been so good to us already."

"Okay, Harry. I understand," Alice told him. "I haven't had my first cup of coffee yet, but I'll get back to you. I'll let the information about Madison sink in and see if I can't get you upstate to see your lovely wife, maybe even tonight. I'm sure she's missing you too. Stay calm."

"Okay, Alice," Harry answered her. "I'm sorry for the inconvenience. Thank you very much. Phil and I are off work Saturday, and we were planning on an outing to the Stadium for a game. I don't even know who the Yankees are playing. You think I should keep the appointment?"

"Absolutely, Harry. Madison could prove useful to us. He's probably the one who took your gun. Let me think about all this. I'll call you at work this afternoon."

He gave Alice his private number.

That night Harry was showered and cologned, on his way upstate, under a blanket in the back of Jim Peters's station wagon. He and Elaine would have only a few hours together before he had to head back to the Bronx. Maybe he could get a little sleep before work in the morning.

In a gray Dodge Coronet, several cars back, NYPD Detective Andy Bennett put his cigarette in the car's ashtray and took a long drink from his flask. He mused about how much he was drinking lately. He would address it, but not right now. It was shaping up to be a long night, and he needed the alcohol and nicotine to keep him awake and alert.

"Finally, I think there's something I can do for Harry. I can get to young Philip," Alice told her three companions at the concession stand. They were taking a food break under the grandstands at Yankee Stadium.

"He will never betray his boss," Jotaro commented. "It would be suicide."

"He's young, full of himself, and dumb," Vargas objected, "an unbeatable combination. I bet Alice can scare him into doing something stupid. Maybe she can even get Applewood's gun back."

Jim paid for everyone's hot dogs and beer.

Alice moved over to the mustard and sauerkraut. She squeezed mustard onto her franks, then used the tongs for the sauerkraut.

"We have to do something pretty soon," she announced, "because, if the other night is any indication, Harry and Elaine are not going to tolerate being apart much longer. They went at it like farm animals when we smuggled him upstate for their conjugal visit. They had no shame. I had to bang on the door over the noise to get them to wrap it up so we could get Harry out of there before daylight."

"Calm down, Alice," Jim told her. "You got pretty excited yourself over the racket they were making. It's a good thing that when we finished dropping Harry off, your apartment was so handy in the same building."

"Jim, please. Could we talk about this some other time?" Alice reddened. "In private?"

"You're the one who brought it up. I only agreed with you that they made quite a lot of noise. I try to be a gentleman at all times, Alice."

"Yeah, well, this time you missed." She attempted to end the exchange.

"Don't be embarrassed on our

account," Vargas commented, indicating him and Jotaro. "We are grown men. We understand such things. Some people can't keep quiet when they engage physically."

"Okay, okay," Alice replied. "Could we talk about something else, for heaven's sake? It was my fault. I admit it. I should learn to keep my mouth shut. Finish fixing your hot dogs, and we'll pay some attention to the problem at hand. We're here to keep an eye on these guys. And watch the game, and make a plan."

Whitey Ford was pitching against the Boston Red Sox. The Yankees had scored the only run of the game in the first inning.

The quartet sat ten rows behind Applewood and Madison, eating their food and sipping beer.

At the bottom of the fourth, in the excitement of the Yankees 'second run, Alice leaned toward Antonio and suggested, "Maybe I should have Harry introduce me to

Madison."

"I don't know, Alice," Vargas replied. "Like in boxing. To make contact, you have to get close enough to be hit. It sounds dangerous. Of course, that's no reason not to do it. What do you have in mind?"

"Are you serious, Antonio?" Alice responded. "I can do something Harry couldn't possibly do. I can make Madison lose his mind with that special weapon we women employ. I will bat my eyelashes at him and ask him to fetch me the gun."

Antonio looked at her, appreciating the confidence she had been exhibiting since their visit to the shooting range. "All right, but do me a favor and ask Jim what he thinks of your idea so that he knows I didn't put you up to it. Not that you need his permission, I understand, just as a courtesy."

Alice turned around and leaned into Jim. "What would you say if I had dinner with Harry and Philip Madison?"

"Alice, you know you don't have to

make those eyes at me. I'm never gonna tell you what to do. Please, be careful."

# CHAPTER 17

## HARRY'S FRIEND

Harry Applewood was the senior inspector at customs. As such, it was his job to fill out the paperwork on the week's cargo. Phil Madison sat reading a newspaper at his desk, smoking cigarettes and kibitzing over his shoulder with his supervisor. Both of them had their uniform jackets off, hanging on the coat tree.

"Phil," Harry told him, "look over this sheet and see if you think the tonnage and the cargo details are accurate on the ships you inspected." He handed the man a stack of typewriter paper.

“Sure, Harry,” Philip replied, taking the forms. “It’s another Friday night in May, and I have nowhere to go. You don’t either, except home to an empty apartment. How’s Elaine’s mother?”

“Not good,” Harry answered curtly, trying to concentrate on the documents in front of him. It was always a test of his ability to focus, having Phil talk to him while he was entering data on these reports.

“Sorry to hear that. What’s wrong with her?” Phil asked.

Harry may have been distracted, but this interrogation did not escape his notice. He composed an answer.

“I’m not sure,” he answered, turning toward Phil, “but it sounded like pneumonia. Elaine called and said it might be another few weeks. I begged her to make it sooner if at all possible.”

Harry looked back down at the work on his desk.

“Sorry to hear that, old boy,” Phil told

him. "I mean, I'm single, and I'm used to going without female companionship for weeks at a time, but you, you're a married man. It must be hard on the old self-control to be separated from your wife for so long." He was bored and wanted to tweak Harry, thinking about the woman Harry had entertained in the warehouse.

Harry was getting irritated by his coworker's phony concern.

The forms in front of him were a blur.

"Yes. It's rough," Harry commented, "but one of our neighbors is going to meet me here for dinner tonight to see if she can cheer me up."

On cue, there was a soft rap on the office door. Phil could make out the shoulder-length dark hair of a woman through the frosted glass panel with INSPECTORS stenciled across the outer surface. He instinctively straightened his tie and rose to open it.

"Well, hello," Philip told the pretty woman on the other side. "You must be

Harry's date. Please come in."

"I'm not exactly a date," Alice replied, smiling pleasantly as she moved past him into the office, self-consciously wafting Prince Matchabelli's most expensive fragrance up his nose. "I'm just a concerned neighbor of his here to make sure he gets a good dinner."

Recovering as best he could from the merciless barrage to his senses, Philip offered, "Have a seat," rolling out his own desk chair for her. "I'm Phil Madison," he said, a question in his voice.

"Thank you," Alice responded, amused by the intended effect of the fragrance on her prey. "Philip was my brother's name."

"No kidding. What do you mean 'was'?"

"He died in Korea."

"Oh. I'm sorry to hear that."

"Not to worry. We had a wonderful childhood together, and he was happy to serve his country. He knew the risk he was taking and was more than willing to take it."

Even though Jotaro had shadowed her into the neighborhood, Alice wore a long raincoat and an oversized floppy hat to cover as much of herself as possible. She had the hat in her hand. Inside the office, she untied the belt and let the coat fall open to reveal a knee-length black skirt and an open-necked white blouse with a cute little vest over it to cover the gun at the small of her back. She wore no makeup and no jewelry. Philip became light-headed at the sight. His pulse rose. He helped her out of her raincoat. Alice feared she had gone too far. He flushed at his loss of composure, pulled himself together, and busied himself, giving her his chair and hanging her hat and coat on the stand. He took a seat on the top of his desk before he fell down.

"If you don't mind me asking, what's your name?" Philip asked her.

"My name is Alice. Harry didn't mention he had such a handsome coworker."

Just as Philip's face had almost returned to its normal color, it flushed again.

It reminded Alice of boxers she had seen at Madison Square Garden, almost recovered from a beating only to be hit again. To Harry's objective eye, it was kind of brutal. Not so to Alice. She was quite cold-blooded about the process, having watched it in the ring many a Saturday night. A left to the face, another left to the face, then, the coup de grâce, a right to the jaw. A slight sheen had developed on Phil's forehead, visible even to Harry's untrained eye. He was impressed with Alice's mastery. Never had he witnessed a woman so coolly dismantle a man. He thought he lacked self-control with women, but Philip made him look like a saint. It didn't matter that Harry knew it was all an act. Alice was getting him excited too, and there wasn't a thing he could do about it. He was sweating. He couldn't believe it.

Phil was busy checking out Alice's left hand, happily noting that it was unencumbered by any rings denoting romantic entanglement.

It would be an understatement to say

that he was smitten. They knew he would be. To Harry, this was murder, pure and simple. Philip, a fellow male, was paralyzed. It wasn't an enjoyable thing to watch.

Harry broke the spell. "If you would just give me a minute to finish what I'm doing, Alice, I'll take you to dinner."

Without skipping a beat, Philip offered, "Would you like some company?"

Alice smiled at him, warmly. "Why, how nice of you to ask," she said, just like the spider to the fly.

That night Jim Peters propped himself against the wall at the head of Alice's bed, reading a book illuminated by a lamp on the bedside stand. Next to the lamp was a glass of milk from which he took an occasional drink.

It was late. He was concerned that Alice was not yet home.

The sound of a key in the lock was a relief.

She dropped her raincoat on the chair in

the foyer and peeked in through the bedroom door.

"My, don't you look nice in your pajama bottoms, with your milk and your book. Very inviting."

She kicked off her shoes.

"Alice. I was worried about you. It's after eleven o'clock. Everything go all right?" he asked her.

"You missed me. I'm so happy," Alice crooned. "I was entirely safe. Jotaro and Harry fell all over themselves protecting me. If that guy, Madison, had tried anything funny, he would have been dead meat."

She braced a foot on the edge of the mattress, grabbed Jim by the ankles, and slid him down the wall until he was flat on his back. She moved up and straddled him with straight arms, then lowered herself and kissed him tenderly.

"I missed you too," she told him.

Jim tried unsuccessfully to hide his irritation.

"Oh, I see." Alice was amused. "You're jealous. I find that very exciting."

She reached over and turned off the lamp.

# CHAPTER 18

## CHESS

Saturday morning.

Alice studied matters of evidence: laying a foundation at trial, determining which facts matter, leading witnesses, and the rules of evidence. She would have to keep it all in mind as she closed in on the union boss, Alfred Menken.

It was a rainy morning in the Bronx. She was seated at her kitchen table with coffee and toast, reading her textbook. The window was open. She watched the rainfall. Jim was still asleep in the bedroom. The night before, she had obliterated his jealousy in a flood of passion. Afterward, they had both slept like babies.

*Let's see,* Alice thought, *leading a witness.*" Good morning, sweetheart," she greeted Jim when he shuffled into the kitchen in a T-shirt and pajama bottoms and poured himself some coffee.

"Let me make you toast." She stood up, relieved to take a break from the tedium of legal protocol. She took two slices of bread from the loaf in the bread box and slid them down in the toaster.

He put his coffee down. "Thanks," he said and wrapped his arms around her.

"Nice," Alice responded. "You brushed your teeth. What a man."

It had been a long time between Jim's divorce and this relationship with Alice. He couldn't get used to this kind of intimacy. He blushed.

"You smell good too," he told her. "You were very nice to me last night when you got home. You were right. I was jealous. I'm sorry. It just got away from me, had a life of its own. There wasn't a thing I could do to stop it. Believe me, I tried. You caught me at it, embarrassed me, and had your way with me. I owe you for that. Thanks."

"I was flattered, Jim. I thought you must be terribly fond of me; though, honestly, you didn't stand a chance. I had on my best perfume, and I was wearing an adorable outfit. Let's face it. I was irresistible. You were putty in my hands. Anyway, you were the one who molested me. I deserved whatever I got. It was amazing. Just give me fifteen more minutes of studying, and I'll make you a proper breakfast. Then you can take me out for a long walk in the rain. I love spring. We could walk over to the botanical gardens, then to the zoo to see the monkeys."

"Fair enough," Jim replied. "I'll grab a shower and leave you to your studies. You look worried. Is everything okay?"

"I feel like this is moving too slow. Harry's in danger. His so-called friend, Philip

Madison, may not be any help at all, and he's a jerk. Even so, we exchanged phone numbers. He may be under too much pressure to do us any good. I don't see how I can sweet-talk him into giving me Harry's gun back or getting me proof that Menken had that man killed, or anything about them smuggling guns through the port. Don't worry about it. Something will develop. The best thing you can do is distract me." She smiled coyly.

Sunday morning.

"Milton, I need your help. I know it's Sunday, but you said to call if I got stuck."

"Sure, Alice," Milt Davis's voice came back over the phone. "I'm glad you called. Life was getting a little dull without hearing about your life-threatening antics."

"How's Elaine doing?"

"Considering her circumstances, your

neighbor is doing quite well. She's a pleasure to have as a guest."

Milton asked her, "Can we discuss this on the phone, or do you need to see me in person?"

"I hate to be a pain, Milton, but would you and Ellen mind coming down and letting me buy you dinner at Luigi's? Anyway, it would be a good time for you to meet my friend at the *Post*, Franklin Jones. I think you and Ellen would really enjoy him. Luigi's opens in the late afternoon on Sundays. Maybe we could sit around over coffee, in my apartment, before dinner, and discuss how much I don't know about what I'm doing. I'm getting nervous. You can do your chess analysis thing, and maybe I can figure out my next move. I've tried, but I'm not getting anywhere, and time's a-wasting."

Milton asked, "How's about Ellen and me mosey down one or two o'clock? Our houseguest will be all right without us for a while. There are leftovers from last night's dinner, and she seems to be in the middle of a book."

Alice answered him, "Good. I'm going to try to get Franklin to come over too. He's a bright guy, and he knows a lot about the politics of the waterfront."

Alice called Jones and asked him to come over if he could make it, which he could. He asked if it would be all right to bring his young girlfriend, Cindy. Alice told him, certainly.

The thought of guests in her place prompted a frenzy of vacuuming and dusting. She and Jim moved the kitchen table into the foyer by the front door since she had no dining room. She took the two sturdiest chairs out of the kitchen and went next door to borrow four folding bridge chairs from a neighbor. She put one of the kitchen chairs at the head of the table for Franklin. Jim took the garbage out to the incinerator chute.

Alice walked across the Concourse and down a side street to the little neighborhood bakery, where she got a dozen fresh rolls and some pastries.

A little after one o'clock, she put her largest percolator on. When it came to a boil, she turned the light down and stuck the coffee basket in.

Milt found a space for his truck on the side street. He and Ellen went in through the basement entrance and took the elevator up. Franklin and his girlfriend, Cindy, walked from the subway station. Alice buzzed open the Concourse door into the lobby for them.

Milt pressed Alice's doorbell. The chimes sounded inside.

"Who's there?" came Alice's muffled voice.

"The milkman." Milton chuckled. "Open up."

Hugs and kisses were exchanged. The Davises took seats at the table. Franklin and his short, gorgeous, very young, very blond girlfriend showed up. He introduced her as Cindy Pinsky. The smell of coffee and bakery products filled the cramped space. There was butter and cream cheese out. Alice poured the coffee and introduced her guests to one another.

"Settle down, Alice," Milt told her. "Stop worrying and pass me the rolls. There's nothing you're dealing with that this brain trust you've gathered in your closet-like apartment can't solve. Watch your elbows, everyone. We don't want any injuries."

Alice handed him the plate piled with hard rolls. He removed one and passed the rest.

"Okay, Milton." Alice took a deep breath. "I feel better already. Maybe the six of us can think of something to get me on track."

"Back away from it, Alice, as I taught you," Milt advised her, "up above the chessboard."

"So, how are your law studies going, Alice?" Ellen interjected, not all that interested in her husband's chess analysis of the shenanigans on the waterfront.

"They're pooping along," Alice answered. "Interestingly, I'm taking a course in Evidence. I would love to have something, anything at all, to present to a court of law, relevant to this case."

"Okay," Milt interjected jovially. "If you ladies will take a short break from gossiping, we can get started. I take it you are familiar with Alice's dilemma, Franklin?"

"Yes," Jones responded, biting into a pastry. "She gave me the gist of her neighbor's situation, and I know something about the man behind his troubles."

"Good," Milt went on, "let's start with who the black pieces are, Alice."

Alice began, "I had my friend Antonio run down the waterfront hierarchy for me. The Black King is clearly Alfred Menken, president of the Dockworkers 'Union, but suspected of other nefarious enterprises. He is reputed to be a very violent man. He's who Johnny Friendly was supposed to be in *On the Waterfront*, only, if my information is correct, Lee J. Cobb played a pale imitation of Menken. Besides being the chief executive of the union, he is rumored to be involved in gunrunning. They say he kind of uses the port as his own personal import–export business. Antonio says he thinks the Irish mob in Hell's Kitchen provides Menken with protection, so we should be careful if and when we decide to extricate our friend, Harry, from his unwilling involvement."

"Excellent. Who's next?"

"I guess Menken's wife, Anna, qualifies as the Black Queen—I initially thought by marriage only, but now I hear she is a force to be reckoned with," Alice explained. "They pretend she doesn't have much to say about his business affairs, but Antonio says we should not underestimate her. She might not be the long-suffering wife they make her out to be. She did pretty well as a smart and ruthless woman on the waterfront before she married Alfred. That could be why he married her."

Alice went on, "The Black Bishop is clearly Menken's right-hand man, Louis Shaughnessy. He conducts most of the union's business operations and Menken's other interests and acts as a buffer to limit his boss's exposure as much as possible. He also, incidentally, controls the notoriously brutal Black Pawns, Irish Pete and Scar, evil men, and tells them what to do, who to hurt, maybe even who to kill."

"Go on," Milt encouraged her.

"Menken has two Black Knights," she said. "One, now deceased, was the late Irving Teleducci, and a second has emerged from under a rock. This one happens to be a young customs inspector named Philip Madison, supervised by my neighbor, Inspector Harold Applewood. We're not sure what his connection with Menken is, but we assume he's the one who broke into Harry's desk and removed his .38 Special, which was, in all probability, used to kill young Irving."

"See how easy that was, Alice. You're doing great," Milt told her. He turned to Franklin Jones and asked him, "You have anything to add so far, Franklin?"

"Not really," Franklin replied. "Alice's friend has more on these people than I have.

I'm jealous. I should get him to work for me. I gotta tell you, I love this approach to the problem. It really sets Applewood's situation in a logical context. Maybe something will come up this way that will move Alice along. When she gives me the go-ahead, and I write my story, chess will be a great framework to put it in. I'm taking mental notes. Please proceed."

"Okay," Milt continued. "Now for the white pieces, Alice."

"Well," Alice started, "there's not half as many of them. I guess the federal government is white, which makes President Eisenhower the White King. That would make Mamie Eisenhower the White Queen and Secretary of Commerce Sinclair Weeks a White Bishop. Inspector Applewood is the other White Bishop, despite the fact he is being coerced into the role of an accomplice to illegal importation, and he's a principal suspect in a murder investigation. The White Knights are the two police officers investigating the murder, Detectives Scott

Gerard and Andrew Bennett, who, Franklin says, are very good at their jobs. That makes me a White Castle, a pain-in-the-neck bystander, meddling in other people's affairs as usual. You're one of our White Pawns, Milton. So are Jim, Antonio, and Antonio's friend Jotaro. You too, Franklin. Maybe we're not so outnumbered after all, if you include the president and the first lady."

"Exactly, Alice," Milt commented. "Just let it all settle in your head. Think about the moves that have already been made and the moves yet to come. Start with just the pieces lined up on the board, at rest for the moment."

Alice asked herself and the room, "What am I overlooking?"

She thought about it. "Obviously, Menken needs Harry Applewood, at least for now. I think it's obvious to everyone that Harry's running out of tolerance for his and his wife's situation, unfortunately, much to Menken's dismay and irritation. He's going to get hurt or killed if we don't find a way to get him out of it soon. The obvious solution would be for him to turn himself in and trust the federal government to protect him, but with this murder rap hanging over his head, Harry's not inclined to take that option, yet."

Franklin said, "He may not have a choice."

"Right now, he thinks he does, since coercion would not be that easy to prove, especially with the large cash deposits he's been making into his bank account, of all places. He is obviously not a career criminal. It would be his word against theirs. Even so, and with his and his wife's lives hanging in the balance, Harry managed to lose his temper, beat up the murder victim, Mr. Teleducci, in front of witnesses, and incur Menken's wrath. If he weren't so difficult to replace, he'd be dead already, shot in the head, on the waterfront, right next to where Irving was killed. Phil Madison must be waiting in the wings, but, thank heaven, he's just inexperienced enough to keep Harry valuable and alive. Considering who Menken is, I wouldn't count on Harry's value much longer. Menken needs to take back control of Applewood or dump him."

"Good, Alice," Milt told her. "So right now, Harry's boxed in. If he insists, I say leave him where he is, but give him protection. Check with your law firm 'cause it's their case. They may disagree. They might want him to turn himself in rather than risk his life. Which black piece do you want to attack first?"

"The weakest link," Alice reflected, "is, without a doubt, Philip Madison. I've already started a little flirtation with him. What do you think, Jim?"

"Don't look at me, Alice. He sounds like he deserves whatever happens to him."

"He's right, Alice," Milt told her. "But we don't want this getting out of hand like what happened last year. Did Antonio take you to the gun range like you said he was going to?"

"Yes, he did, and it was a revelation.

I'm sorry I waited so long. So, I'm going to create a panic in little Philip. That ought to keep him out of a romantic mood."

Alice concluded, "I'm feeling much better about what I'm doing. I suppose I might have worked this out by myself, but then I would have missed dinner with my wonderful friends."

"At this rate, you and your firm are gonna go broke, Alice," Milt told her, "but I could never resist a bribe."

Cindy Pinsky finally spoke up. "I love Luigi's, Miss White. My dad brought me there when I was small, and I never forgot it. I hope you don't mind Franklin bringing me here today. I liked hearing you talk about your work. I'm an actress, and I can never get enough character material, watching other women do their jobs. I hope I see you again."

"How sweet," Alice responded. "I'm so happy you came, Cindy. Please call me Alice. Let's get together sometime to chat. Let's stay in touch."

“Yes, Alice,” Franklin added. “Let’s do that. And call us for help anytime. This was very exciting, watching you organize your investigation. I may write a whole book about it, call it *Chess Master of Murder*. I might even write a screenplay, get Marlon Brando to play Harry and Karl Malden to play Milton. Let’s head to the restaurant. I’m hungry.”

Cindy Pinsky and Franklin left Luigi’s to head back downtown.

The next day she and Alice met for lunch in a midtown sandwich shop. They took a booth. The place, like most such operations in that area, was packed.

“How nice of you to meet me, Alice. I so enjoyed our visit to your apartment yesterday. I didn’t want to interrupt the business you were doing with Franklin and Mr. Davis. I was serious about how watching you do your job would be good for my acting career."

"Well, how nice. We girls have to look after each other. I'm glad to help you any way I can."

"I've had a pretty sheltered life, Alice. I grew up in the Bronx, and I went to an all-girls high school, Walton. My parents were from Poland, barely spoke English. They were nervous and very protective of me. In fact, if it hadn't been for the desperation of Walton's drama coach, I would never have become interested in acting. She had me play men's parts and women's too. Anyone willing was welcome to be in the school plays. Some of us were terrible, but I wasn't too bad, and I liked the costumes and pretending to be other people. So I decided not to go to college, got a job as a waitress, and enrolled in an acting workshop."

"How interesting, Cindy," Alice commented. "It never occurred to me to go on the stage. I grew up in Queens. I was a tomboy and hung out with my older brother's friends. Philip died in Korea."

"Gee, Alice. I'm sorry."

"Nah, it's okay. He wanted to serve his country, and it's the chance he took. I miss him, though. It's only been a few years, but I'm still a tomboy; I lost my job at a department store in New Jersey to a returning GI when the Second World War was over. So, I decided to become a career woman of a different sort, a lawyer. I couldn't afford to go to law school without a day job. That's why I work at a law firm on the seedy side of Nassau Street as a secretary. They promoted me to a legal assistant, but I couldn't escape who I was. Now, I run their investigations. I turned out to have a talent for it, like you and acting, and I'm still going to law school at night."

"I don't know if I'd call myself a talented actress, Alice. I have an agent, Ray Vincent, who's supposed to get me work, but he's more interested in using me to be with producers and big shots so that he can promote his more important clients. It's the story of my life. He got into my pants, and he got these important men in there too, and now, he only ever books me for TV ads and bit parts on Broadway. That's how Franklin and I met. He and his ex-wife were out with his boss from the paper, and he sat in the front row, staring up at my legs. I was a secretary sitting at a desk at the edge of the stage. He was cute, I must say. He and his wife were about to end their marriage. He drinks too much. Sorry. That's not a thing to say to a friend of his."

"Yeah, Cindy, I'm already well aware that he does, and neither do I want to insult him by bringing it up."

"He's been so good to me, Alice. He wants me to move in with him, but we have different work schedules, and, frankly, his drinking does not fit into my style of life. We go out to dinner a lot. He's really a brilliant man. I love hearing him talk. He's like an encyclopedia. He knows so much about everything. I can see why you like him too. You're as smart as he is, and you're beautiful too. He loves pretty ladies. I'm glad he has you in his life. He's great fun until he gets sleepy. That's when I bring him home and tuck him in. I hope I don't sound ungrateful, Alice."

"No, Cindy, just realistic. That's what it takes to get by as a woman these days. Frankly, I am glad he has someone like you in his life too. You are brilliant yourself, and you deserve some success. You don't sound like you need career advice. I'll bet you will find a way to better your situation."

"Thank you, Alice. By the way, I'd love it if you let me know how you're doing with the case you're working on. It sounds like that union boss is a pretty awful man. I hope you get him."

"I do too," Alice replied. "Give me your number, and I'll call you."

Cindy stopped to use the phone at a drugstore on her way further downtown.

She had another benefactor besides

Franklin Jones. This one stayed awake for the lovemaking portion of their evenings together.

"Hello, Louis. I'm fine, just fine. I had lunch with your inspector's neighbor, Alice White. She promised to let me know how things are going with that mean old union boss, Alfred Menken. She's trying to pin that murder on him."

Thanks to Cindy, Louis Shaughnessy now knew all about Applewood's neighbor, Alice White, and her relationship to Harry and his wife, Elaine. Now, he also knew about their so-called weak link, Philip Madison, and the plan to use him against his Uncle Alfred.

Since the conference in Alice's apartment, Cindy couldn't help but think of herself as a Trojan horse, a Black Knight, painted white, for Franklin's friends to play with.

# CHAPTER 19

## FUNERAL HOME

There was an unusual source of culinary competition with the popular neighborhood Italian restaurant, Luigi's. It was Cavuto's Funeral Home. Just like at a firehouse, there is a significant amount of downtime in the undertaking business. Like many firefighters, Roberto Cavuto used the breaks to refine his kitchen skills.

A pot of tomato sauce simmered daily on the stove in his kitchen.

Roberto was sixty, short, with a fringe of gray hair circling the top of his shiny head. Bags hung under his eyes. Red suspenders draped over his prominent abdomen. The mournful expression of his profession adorned his face.

Cavuto's lovely wife, Tina, was the opposite in temperament. She was animated and affectionate. She often snuck into the kitchen to taste his sauce. She would impishly throw in more oregano, salt, or rosemary, to get a rise from her husband. He dutifully took exception, as she knew he would, and they engaged in playful argument, subdued so as not to disturb any mourners on the premises. Roberto never allowed his protests to threaten the peace of their marriage or their business. They had created a tranquil environment where loved ones could grieve in peace. If the deceased's family were personal friends, they would be invited into the kitchen for a special treat. Roberto would pour homemade red wine for them into water glasses from a jug balanced on his shoulder.

It was noon.

"Manny," Roberto exclaimed when he

spotted the pharmacist entering his darkened foyer through the front door. “How nice to see you. Come into the kitchen, and I’ll fix ya a nice plate a spaghetti for lunch.”

“It’s good to be here, Roberto,” Manny replied to his friend.

Roberto pushed open the kitchen door. Manny was immediately enveloped in the smell of garlic and herbs. He settled in at the unfinished kitchen table while Roberto put some water on to boil and salted it. The undertaker took out a dinner plate, retrieved the jug of red wine from its cabinet, and poured some for Manny and himself as well.

“To what do I owe the pleasure?” Roberto asked. “Ya know, Manny, ya never need an excuse ta visit Tina and me. Ya always make us laugh.”

Manny smiled broadly and raised his glass in salutation. Roberto toasted Manny back, and they drank.

“Thank you, Roberto,” Manny told his friend. “I always enjoy visiting. You and Tina are such a great audience for my jokes. I won't lie to you. Your pasta is also incredible. But, I do have a reason to be here this time."

"Anything, Manny," Roberto told him. "Anything at all. You have been so good to me. You're always cheerful when I wake you up in the middle of the night to work with me in those tricky situations. You take a risk helping me with my clients; I mean the ones that aren't dead yet, helping me patch them up. I appreciate it. What can I do for you?"

Roberto glanced over at the pot of water and could see small bubbles rising to the surface. He took the lid off a tin canister, lifted out a fistful of spaghetti, and put it on the plate by the stove. He turned back to his guest with a raised brow.

"Roberto," Manny spoke when he had his host's attention, "one of my customers up there on the Concourse is in trouble. Maybe you can help him. I don't know. You have friends with connections on the West Side of Manhattan, right?"

"Sure, Manny. I have friends here in

the Bronx with influence on the waterfront. A lot of us are moving there from the old country. What dya need?" Roberto asked him.

"This man is a customs inspector," Manny told him. "He's in some jam. I don't know exactly, but it's not hard to guess it has to do with what he does for a living. He's looking at prison time, and I guess they're threatening to hurt his wife."

"Hmm." Roberto sighed. "We try and stay outta their business at the waterfront. It is mostly them Micks, right now, but that can change. Who knows? My countrymen might want to talk with your friend. In fairness to the Irish, Manny, about your friend, ya gotta do what ya gotta do to make a living. Capisce?"

"Yes, Roberto," Manny responded. "I understand. Business is business. I appreciate that. But, with all due respect, they're ruining my friend's life. They stole his gun and it looks like they killed someone with it. The man will be stripped of his profession, his money will be taken away from him, and he'll go to prison, maybe even be executed for the murder he didn't commit. I believe in making a dollar just like anyone else, but this is a high price for an innocent man and his wife to pay."

Roberto slid the spaghetti off the plate, into the boiling water. Manny looked on in anticipation, then finished his remaining wine.

Roberto refilled his glass.

Manny exclaimed, "Whoa, Roberto. I have to get back to my store. I don't want to fall asleep before I go home tonight."

"Dat's what strong coffee is for, Manny. Don't worry. I'll straighten ya out before ya leave."

Roberto reached up to the cabinet and took down two shallow wooden bowls. He pulled out a drawer, took out two forks and two soup spoons, and set the table.

"I'll sniff around and see what I can find out," he commented. "It's a delicate balance down there. The Irish consider us interlopers. Do you like that word, interlopers? I just learned it. I read it in the newspaper. But time marches on. Maybe there's room for a new arrangement. Italians are pouring into the whole West Side. And dem Puerto Ricans, they're moving in too. Geez, they're a tough bunch, cut their own sista's throat for a fix. I can't promise you anything, but I'll see what I can do, without getting your friend hurt, if possible."

"Is your boss in?" Cavuto asked on the phone. "It's Roberto Cavuto. I want to talk to him today if he could give me some time. I'll hold on while you see.

"Okay, sure. I'll be there in an hour."

Enzo Trusgnich sat like a ramrod, sipping espresso in the back office of his men's club off Arthur Avenue, the Little Italy of the Bronx. In his seventies, he was the eldest of the New York–New Jersey Italian bosses. Black-haired young guards took turns sitting on a chair inside the front door of the building, a shotgun across their lap, their right hand resting on the polished stock.

Between sips, Enzo listlessly flipped through the daily Neapolitan newspaper he had delivered, *Il Mattino.*

He detected the fading odor of sausage, peppers, and onions from last night's dinner, prepared in the adjacent kitchen. It went well with the aroma of his espresso. He remembered the meal and managed the slightest hint of what passed, on his rigid face, for a smile.

There was a soft knock on the door before it opened. It was Salvatore Bonazzi, Trusgnich's trusted lieutenant.

"Mr. T.," Salvatore spoke through the half-open door. "Mr. Cavuto is here. Can I bring him in?"

Enzo nodded his assent.

Trusgnich stood and embraced his old

comrade.

Roberto presented the customs inspector's case. Harry Applewood was the man's name. He asked if Applewood could be helped.

"I'll take a look and see what I can do," Trusgnich told Cavuto. "He's in the middle of something that's already happening between the Irish and us, and he doesn't even know it. It isn't going well. The potato-eaters are not embracing change. We might have a use for your guy. Maybe we could do him some good in turn. I won't lie to you, Roberto. He's in a dangerous spot."

"I know you will do what you can, my friend," Cavuto told him before he left.

The next day, in the same room: "Pasquale is here to speak to you." Salvatore never expected an audible response from his boss.

Enzo, wearing a freshly laundered white shirt, with a new *Il Mattino* on the table and a fresh cup of espresso next to it, tilted his head and gave Salvatore an affirmative blink.

Bonazzi opened the door further. From behind him, a strong-looking young Italian man stepped into the room, hat in hand.

"Sit," Trusgnich told him.

Salvatore closed the door on his way out.

"So, Pasquale?" Trusgnich asked the man.

"You already know, they're bringing guns in through the port," Pasquale Mazetti told him. "Their business is mostly guns right now."

Pasquale had worked long and hard on his English pronunciation. Salvatore had told him when he got the job that Mr. T. insisted on good American English. Pasquale was from the Bay of Naples, like the boss, and like Salvatore. He glanced down at the *Il Mattino* Mr. Trusgnich was reading and felt a twinge of homesickness. He missed his widowed mother. His sadness quickly evaporated under the cold glare of the older man.

The door opened. Salvatore entered to listen, shut the door, and sat down.

Trusgnich spoke. “Tell me how the customs thing works?”

“They have one inspector in the open, Mr. Trusgnich,” Pasquale began, “and they got another inspector watching him.”

Pasquale swallowed half his little cup of espresso.

“That’s good to know, in case something happens to the main guy,” Enzo exclaimed. “We’re gonna have to talk with him. His name is Applewood. You know where he lives?”

“Yeah,” Pasquale answered. “He’s not far from here, on the Concourse.”

“Okay,” Trusgnich told him. “Wait outside.”

Trusgnich’s face never changed expression. It was cold as winter. He sat perfectly still, his back rigid.

Pasquale slid his chair back and stood. Hat in hand, he bowed slightly at the waist to Trusgnich, backed partially out of the room, turned, and left.

When the door was closed, Enzo told Salvatore, “This is gonna get messy. The Irish ain’t gonna take this lying down. It was bound to happen.”

“I know, boss,” Salvatore responded stoically.

“This customs man’s problem is just what we need to get a foot in the door. Let’s have a meeting of our friends from Manhattan and New Jersey before the blood begins to spill. When we have an agreement, you can bring the inspector to me for a talk.”

# CHAPTER 20

## AT THE WALDORF

In 1931 the Waldorf Astoria moved from Fifth Avenue to Park Avenue. The Empire State Building was erected on its original site. The new Waldorf became an art deco landmark.

The hotel on Park Avenue had its own railway platform, a siding from Grand Central Station, famously used by President Franklin Roosevelt and General Douglas MacArthur. Gatherings, both famous and infamous, were held within its walls. One of the infamous ones was held in the spring of 1956, in a penthouse suite with a magnificent New York City view. Attending were Adolfo Drago of

Newark, New Jersey, Angelo Benedetto from Manhattan, and Enzo Trusgnich from the Bronx, along with their entourages.

Cannolis—originally from Drago's Sicilian hometown—other pastries, cheeses, plates of fresh fruit, pots of Savarin coffee, pitchers of ice water, silver cups of creamer, and bowls of sugar were clustered on a table in the living room. Cups and saucers, plates, silverware, and white linen napkins were also laid out. The servers were generously tipped and dismissed. They had looked at the attendees' supporting staff when they arrived to inspect the premises before the conference. These were intense, brutal-looking men. It was not difficult for the maids and stewards to discern that they were armed and capable of great violence. They were all grateful to have been excused.

Drago and Benedetto sat at opposite ends of the couch, separated by several yards of frigid air. They left the comfort of the lone upholstered armchair on the other side of the coffee table to their esteemed elder colleague from the Bronx.

The bodyguards sat in straight-backed chairs, off to the side of the room, ready to move at a moment's notice.

Angelo Benedetto stood and took a gold cigarette case from the side pocket of his suit. His bodyguard stood simultaneously. Benedetto was sixty-three years old, with chiseled Italian features, neatly combed white hair, and dark eyes. He was muscular and trim. His suit was black silk with a black silk tie and a red handkerchief sticking out of the breast pocket. He removed a cigarette from the case, closed it, and tamped the cigarette on its face. His bodyguard moved his considerable bulk across the carpet, and, as Benedetto seated the cigarette in his mouth, the man lifted a Ronson from the coffee table and lit it. He placed a clean ashtray next to the lamp at his boss's end of the couch and returned to his chair.

Benedetto took a puff, exhaled, and started. "Gentlemen. Welcome to my office at the Waldorf. I hope you're comfortable. I'm glad we could all make it."

The short, round Adolfo Drago, from New Jersey, pressed his lips together in a cold smile and nodded his head once in the affirmative, without looking at Benedetto. Drago's hair had a bad black dye job greased and combed over his head's bald top. His mustache was likewise dyed black. He wore a blue pinstipe suit, with no pocket-handkerchief. His suspenders, stretched over his round stomach, could be seen peeking out from behind his open jacket.

Enzo Trusgnich wore neither a jacket nor a tie. He had on black slacks with an expensive-looking leather belt and a white linen shirt, buttoned at the neck. He sat rigidly and still, gave a glance with his dead eyes in acknowledgment, then gazed back into space.

"Adolfo, my friend," Benedetto went on, "I take it you have spoken with your associates in Newark and Trenton about this matter."

Adolfo Drago uncrossed his legs.

Benedetto was not his friend. Benedetto was from Rome. He, Drago, was from Palermo, in Sicily. He deliberately lifted the cup and saucer from the table beside him, crooked his little finger, and took a sip. Then he replaced the coffee on the table beside him.

After the dramatic pause, he spoke with a thick Italian accent, "Yes, I 'ave talked wit dem. Dey is agreeable with hearing what we have to say after this meeting is over. They too think it's time to redistribute the wealth of the Port a New York, the port that we in Jersey share with your great city."

Trusgnich lifted his malevolent gaze to Drago but said nothing. How long had Drago lived in America? Wasn't it time he learned to speak the language?

*He still sounds like the poor immigrant he was when he got off the boat,* Trusgnich thought. *He's the kind of scungilli that gives Italians a bad name. Next time he should bring an interpreter.*

"And you, Enzo?" Benedetto knew better than to call Trusgnich his friend.

Trusgnich had grown up close to where Al Capone had once lived. The two had been close until Capone died of a stroke in 1947 a complication of his lifelong battle with syphilis. Trusgnich made Capone look like a choirboy. "How do you feel?"

"Okay," Trusgnich answered. "Don't worry about my health. The Bronx is interested in a piece of this Irish pie, so let's get to cutting."

Both the other men were aware of Trusgnich's reputation with a knife. They shuddered.

The next evening, a white panel van with CITY CARPET CLEANING stenciled on its side parked outside the basement entrance of Alice's apartment building. Two men in overalls got out and went in through the unlocked gate.

Alice thought she'd check on her neighbor, Harry Applewood. He was isolated in his apartment and worried about the future. She pulled her blouse out to cover the automatic nestled in the small of her back and left her apartment.

"Hi, Alice," Harry greeted her. "Come on in."

"How're you holding up, Harry?" she asked when she saw him standing in the doorway.

"As well as can be expected."

When they were safely inside, he added, quietly, "As well as can be expected with my wife on the lam and me waiting for the ax to fall. Want some coffee?"

"Yes, please. Thank you."

They sat at the kitchen table.

"I'm sorry this isn't moving any faster," Alice told him. "Hang in there. We did well with your partner, Phil, the other night. He's my next project. I expect him to call me anytime now. Then I'll turn the screws on him, and he will suddenly lose his appetite for my company, but by that time, it will be too late. In the meantime, I'll try to get you up to visit Elaine again as soon as I can, but I don't want to endanger her in the process by accidentally leading someone up there."

"I'm okay, really, Alice," Harry told her. "Let's hold off on another visit and concentrate on getting us out of danger. I'm beginning to think that going to the feds is what I should do."

The bell rang. Harry got up to answer it. He hadn't buzzed anyone into the building's front entrance, but delivery people often came in by way of the unlocked basement.

"Who's there?" he asked through the locked and chained door.

"City Carpet," a man answered. "We have an order to pick up a carpet for cleaning."

Harry unlocked the door and looked through the small space the chain allowed.

He told the two men, "My wife must have arranged this before she left to see her family."

Harry closed the door, unchained it, and opened it for the men to come in. The men entered and closed the door behind them.

"There's only one carpet that needs cleaning," Harry said. "That must be the one she called you about. It's in the living room, right there." Harry pointed into the sunken living room, two shallow steps down from the foyer.

One of the men slid a .45 out of the side pocket of his overalls. There was a bulky attachment on the end, which, Harry surmised, must be a silencer. He froze.

"Just lay down on the carpet, and we'll take you with it," the man told Harry.

Alice drew her gun, slid the safety off, and moved to the kitchen door, her finger on the trigger.

Harry, worried about Alice, instinctively twitched his head toward the kitchen.

Alice heard *pffft* and felt a searing sensation in her right arm as soon as she reached the doorway. The Browning dropped out of her hand and hit the floor. In two strides, one of the gunmen was on her, backhanded his weapon across the side of her head, and turned her lights out.

Frankie the window washer stood on the fire escape outside the customs man's bedroom window, used a screwdriver to open the catch, and slipped into the apartment. He stepped quietly down the hallway to the foyer where Alice lay unconscious, a bruise on the side of her face and her arm pumping blood into a puddle on the floor. He pushed her sleeve up and wrapped his handkerchief tightly around her arm above the wound, tight enough to stop the bleeding.

Alice awoke to the nauseating smell of formaldehyde. Her head ached. Her right arm was on fire. She looked up from the table to see the kindly face of the pharmacist, Manny Harrison, looking back at her.

"Hi, Alice. How're you feeling?"

"Not good, Manny. Where am I?"

"Don't be alarmed when I tell you this, but you're in the funeral home on Wilbert Avenue, down the hill, behind your building."

Alice looked over and saw a rather chubby, balding gentleman she recognized from the bocce ball games in the lot after church on Sundays. His shirtsleeves were rolled up, and there was blood on the front of his shirt—her blood, she supposed.

"This is Mr. Cavuto," Manny told her. "He's the owner. He cleaned the bullet track in your arm and stopped the bleeding."

"It was just a flesh wound, as they say in the business," Cavuto informed her. "It did nick the artery, but thanks to a tourniquet, the bleeding was controlled. It was a big bullet, a .45, from the looks of it. You're lucky. It missed most of the important structures in your arm."

"How'd I get here?" Alice asked him.

"Frankie brought you," Cavuto told her.

"Frankie who?" she asked.

"Frankie. You know him. 'Frankie Windows. 'He's the guy who washes the windows for people in your building."

"Frankie the window washer? How on earth did he find me?"

"He and his boys have been watching your building. They saw two strange men go in the basement and followed them up to your neighbor's place. I'm afraid they got away with your friend. You, unfortunately, were in the wrong place at the wrong time."

"Frankie? He's just a window washer. Why would he be watching my building?" Alice questioned him.

"Ask him next time you see him," Cavuto told her, amused by her ignorance of

Frankie's principal calling.

Manny Harrison handed Alice two small old-fashioned cardboard prescription boxes. One had "#1" inked by hand on its label. The other said "#2."

"Number one is penicillin. Take two of them every six hours until they're gone," he told her. "If you miss a dose, take four. Number two is a narcotic pain pill. Take two of those when you need them for pain, up to every four hours or so. They'll make you drowsy, so don't drive while you're on them."

"I think I'll keep those for an emergency," Alice told him. "If it's okay with you, I'll just take some aspirin for the pain."

"It's okay with me, Alice," Manny replied. "Some people have a higher tolerance for pain than others, but at least take two of them now with your penicillin to take the edge off. In a few hours, your head and your arm are gonna hurt worse than you think. Aspirin's not a bad idea after that, but pay attention 'cause it might make the wound bleed. It'll be messy, but it will help keep it clean. Roberto only closed the track loosely so it can drain out and heal from the inside."

Manny went over to the sink and got Alice a paper cup of water. He handed it to her. She reluctantly took two tablets from each box.

"What is this room?" Alice asked Cavuto. "It smells like chemicals."

"It's my embalming room," he told her, grinning playfully. "It's handy for this kind of thing."

She raised her eyebrows.

"What?" he questioned her. "Is it so strange? I work on people in here. True, they're mostly dead when I do, but a body's a body."

Harry rolled across the floor of a vehicle inside the confines of his living room carpet. After fifteen or twenty minutes, he was carried from the vehicle, laid on a floor, and unrolled. The two men helped him stand up.

"Where am I?" Harry asked.

No answer. They sat him on the edge of a cot and began re-rolling the empty carpet.

"Espresso?" one of them asked Harry.

"Sure," Harry replied. "I guess."

"I'll put a little something in it," the same man told him. When he saw the expression on Harry's face, he added, "Liquor, I mean," and left the room.

The other guy sat on a straight-backed chair, leafing through what looked to Harry like an Italian newspaper.

Judging from his time inside the carpet, Harry guessed they were still in the Bronx, not that far from his apartment building. He smelled tomatoes and garlic. It must be somebody's house or the back of a restaurant, he thought.

The other man returned carrying a saucer with a small cup on it filled with black aromatic liquid. He handed it to Harry and left the room. Harry took a sip. It tasted like coffee and licorice. Rat poison or anisette. He guessed anisette. It was sweet. He did not have to be told. If they wanted to kill him, he'd be dead already.

He remembered the silenced gunshot and wondered if Alice was okay.

"Did you kill her? The woman who was with me," Harry asked.

The paper reader looked up. "Nah, I shot her in the arm. I'm pretty sure she was gonna shoot us. I had to. She's lucky I didn't kill her. The boss'll be in to talk to you. Just sit quiet and have your espresso," he told him and got back to reading the newspaper.

The other man returned a few minutes later and motioned his partner out of the chair. A thin older man with a face like chiseled ice walked into the room and sat down on the chair. One of the kidnappers closed the door and leaned against the wall next to his partner.

The older man fixed Harry in his glare. His face was expressionless, his spine rigid. When he spoke, it was a rasp. "Mr. Applewood, I'm Enzo Trusgnich. Relax."

"Okay."

"You got yourself in a mess with your Irish friends on the docks," the old man wheezed at him. "Where's your wife?"

"Somewhere safe," Harry replied defiantly.

"Okay, okay. That's good enough for now. You're shaking. Have another sip of espresso."

Harry took a swallow.

"Maybe we can do each other some good," Trusgnich told him.

# CHAPTER 21

## THE FLYING IRISHMAN

On February 14, 1945, Valentine's Day, the Royal Air Force of Great Britain and the United States Army Air Forces conducted their second day of raids on Dresden, Germany. These constituted the infamous firebombing of Dresden. They succeeded in killing twenty-five thousand civilians and destroying what many people said was the most beautiful city on the face of the earth.

Freddie Quinn was a college student in 1942 at Western Kentucky State Teachers College.

"Mom, Dad," he told his parents. "This morning, I enlisted in the air force."

"We'd hate to lose you, son, so for God's sake, be careful."

After surviving pilot training, Freddie flew his B-17 bomber and crew over Berlin, Cologne, Essen, and Hamberg to drop their ordnance. Contrary to the popular movie image, they did not have their own personal aircraft with Betty Grable in a swimsuit painted on the fuselage. Planes were assigned on the day of a mission. They took what they were given.

On Valentine's Day, Freddie and his crew ran out of luck over Dresden. Their plane was irreparably damaged. They were forced to bail out. Eight of his nine crew members made it down alive. The ball-turret gunner was shot and killed before he hit the ground. The surviving crew members were taken prisoner but reported missing In action, presumed dead. A few months later, just days before the war was over, Freddie and his crew were liberated by an armored division out of

Fort Knox, Kentucky, and handed over to the Red Cross for transport home.

Freddie was welcomed back to college and got his degree. He subsequently attended Fordham Law School, in New York City, on the GI Bill. His tuition and textbooks were paid for, and he received a whopping $75 a month for living expenses, forcing him to work as an auto mechanic in the evening. During law school, he took an interest in labor law.

There was another Irish law student in Freddie's class. His name was Clarence Eaton. They became good friends and drinking companions.

"I'm fascinated by these labor leaders and what they've accomplished against all odds," Freddie told his friend. "Walter Reuther of the United Auto Workers, John L. Lewis, Jimmy Hoffa, Eugene Debs. They've all made their mark, and, despite some bad actions they've taken, they have managed to achieve some measure of respect for our workforce."

"Yes, they have," his friend commented.

"I'll tell you, though, who really aggravates me, Clarence, is this clown Alfred Menken. He's president of the Dockworkers ' Union at the Port of New York. He's supposed to be sticking up for his members, but instead, he takes advantage of them. He's getting money from shipping companies and his members alike. He's got those men paying him to get work. He's brought corruption to a whole new level, even using the port to smuggle contraband into the country. He's setting the labor movement back a hundred years. I hate this guy."

Quinn could never break through the wall of silence surrounding Menken.

"Hey, Freddie," Clarence Eaton spoke to his old classmate on the phone. "How are you? I have a problem I thought you maybe could help me with. It involves your good buddy, Alfred Menken."

Jim Peters's expansive residence was on the tenth floor of a commercial building near Broadway in Manhattan.

Alice slept propped up on pillows against his headboard. Her legs were under the covers. She awoke to the smell of coffee. Her head ached, and her arm burned. She reached for the cup with her left hand and took a sip.

"Want some eggs, Alice?" Jim stuck his head around the doorjamb. He caught a glimpse of her face and added, "Want some of your pain pills?"

"Yes, please," Alice told him. "I need some relief."

She went on, "You know, I can cook. I'm not exactly helpless. It's just a flesh wound."

"You sound like John Wayne." Jim smiled. "You've got to be hurting. Come on. I have you at my mercy. Face it. Your bosses gave you time off to recuperate. You are all mine to take care of."

"Okay, okay. Don't forget to make toast."

He disappeared, brought back a glass of water and pills.

"It's for you." Jim brought Alice the phone on its long cord from the living room.

"Alice, this is Jotaro Sarisoto. Your neighbor is back at work."

"Terrific. Thanks for calling me. Could you give him a message?"

"Yes, sure."

"Let him know I'm alive and well. If you would, give him this number and tell him I'll be here for a while, and would he call me."

"Okay. I'll take care of it."

"Thanks, Jotaro. Thanks for everything you're doing to keep Harry and me alive."

"No need to thank me, Alice White. I owe Antonio my life, and he owes you his."

Jim and Alice were on the sofa, her feet in his lap. She was reading law; Jim, a book on the inside story of questionable hygiene practices in New York City's restaurants written by a disgruntled, out-of-work chef. How Jim found these books, Alice had no idea.

The phone rang. Jim answered and handed it to Alice. "It's Harry."

"Thanks for calling, Harry. Are you okay?"

"Yes, actually. I am," Harry answered. "How about you? God, I thought they killed you."

"Me? I'm fine, really. He got me in the arm. It's just a flesh wound. It's really not a problem."

She glanced at Jim. He rolled his eyes at her and shook his head in amusement, then resumed reading his book.

"You know," Alice continued on the phone. "I'm a modern woman. We are as tough as nails. What happened to you?"

"They took me somewhere in the Bronx. It was an Italian neighborhood. They made me espresso, and I talked to their boss. He's a scary-looking old guy. They said they would help me if I help them. Maybe I won't go to jail or fry in the electric chair after all, but I'm not counting on these people for anything. I'm sorry you got hurt, really."

"I have a guardian angel," Alice told him. "You know him, I bet. The window washer, Frankie, a man of many faces. He broke into your apartment after they took you away and kept me from bleeding to death. It's a long story, but let's say that a man, who was definitely not a doctor, cleaned the bullet wound, and our corner druggist gave me antibiotics and pain pills. I'll tell you all about it when I see you. So, what do I tell my lawyers?"

"Tell them I'm going along with their plan for now," Harry answered her, "but, if they think I shouldn't, I'll take their advice. Considering they're offering to help me, I figure I should listen to them. Anyway, I'm tired of doing nothing while my life falls apart. My wife is in hiding. This Italian guy, the boss, asked me where she was like I'd tell him, but he didn't get angry when I refused to say. So, I'm gonna do what he asks for now, also, which is to help them cut in on the Irish operation."

Alice told him, "I'm gonna talk to my bosses and see if there's a way we can get you out of that whole scene, sooner rather than later. I'm hoping we can do it in a way that doesn't leave you looking over your shoulder for the rest of your life."

"When this is all over," Harry commented, "I'll be a relatively poor man. The government is no doubt going to take back what's left of my ill-gotten gains. If I don't go to prison, I'll have to get another job. I saw a waiter the other night when Phil and I were out to dinner. I thought about that for a job. Maybe I'll go to work at a car wash. I may not be able to pay you much for your heroic effort."

"Harry, don't worry. I have about a year of law school left before I graduate. Since this is contributing to my professional education, I might end up owing you money. Let's see how it goes."

In spring and summer, Alice's southern Italian neighbors played bocce ball after Mass on Sundays. They gathered in a vacant lot well below the Concourse sidewalk's level, adjacent to the Catholic church. Women in black attended the men, setting up a card table with glasses, crooked cigars, anisette, and red wine. They scattered folding wooden chairs around it. When Mass was over, the men walked down the steep dirt path, hung their jackets and ties over the chairs' backs, and rolled up their sleeves. They sat smoking, gossiping, and sipping wine or anisette while their comrades threw balls. One man threw out the object ball, the Bocchino, and the others tried to get closest to it.

One of the women in black walked to the garden of a house abutting the lot, harvested tomatoes from the vine, and took them inside to cut them up with mozzarella for the men to snack on, but not to ruin their appetites for Sunday dinner.

Alice, Jim, Jotaro, and Antonio balanced themselves on the three-railed black iron fence at the edge of the Concourse sidewalk above the lot. It gave them an aerial view of the game, balls being thrown and men heckling each other in Italian.

"We might as well be living in Italy," Alice proclaimed.

Whenever they were in the Bronx on the weekend and it wasn't raining, she brought Jim here.

Roberto Cavuto spotted Alice from the dirt tract beneath her dangling feet.

"How's the patient?" he asked up at her.

"Fine, thanks. I wouldn't miss your

game for the world."

"Hurt much, Alice?" Cavuto asked her.

"It's bearable," she answered. "I'm taking the penicillin like you said. My head hurts more than my arm. You did a fine job, Mr. Cavuto. Thank you."

"It's nothing. I'm glad to see you up and around. You have been sitting up there for years watching us play. I noticed you a long time ago, though I didn't know who you were. You're a beautiful woman, distracting to our game, in fact, but now, my friends aren't happy when you're not there to watch them. They like to show off for you."

"Thank them for me." Alice reddened. "It's my little taste of Italy in the Bronx."

"There are a few men down here who would be glad to take you back to Italy next time they go; it's just, I wouldn't trust them, Alice. You know about Italian men. You're safer in America. Sometime when you're feeling better, you can come down here. I'll introduce you around, and we'll give you some anisette and a cigar. It'll make their day."

"The cigar would probably kill me. I can smell them from up here. But I'd love to take you up on the anisette when my head hurts a little less."

"Stick around after the game, please?" Cavuto asked her. "I want to look at your arm. In an hour, maybe. Come to my place. Bring your friends. They can have some pasta and taste my latest sauce. It should be perfect if my wife hasn't adjusted it too much. I'll water down some wine so you can have a little. It'll be good for you, keep your strength up."

"We'll be there," Jim, Jotaro, and Antonio responded in unison.

Two hours later, they were all seated in Cavuto's kitchen. He had removed the stitches from Alice's arm, irrigated the wound, and changed the bandage.

Wooden bowls sat in front of each of them, along with forks and spoons. Small tumblers of red wine sat next to their bowls. Alice's was pink.

In a white apron, Cavuto stood at the stove, stirring the sauce with a long wooden spoon.

"I heard about the trouble your neighbor is in, Alice," he said over his shoulder. "Manny, the druggist, visited me. I have connections who said they might be of some help to him, but they're not sure. He's in the middle of a dangerous situation. It was my fault you got shot. That was them that took Mr. Applewood. They like to scare people before they talk business with them. It was nothing personal."

"Oh, Mr. Cavuto," Alice told him, "please don't blame yourself. Getting shot was my fault. I was going to shoot those men. My neighbor thinks you may have done him a favor. He says anything is better than how he's been living. I appreciate your help, even if it doesn't end up making things better for him. At least you tried."

"I'm just saying," Cavuto told her,

"when I get someone shot, my medical services are on the house. Your arm looks pretty good. It cleaned up nice, but, still, finish the penicillin. You know, you're gonna have a scar."

"In that case," Alice replied, "I won't enter any swimsuit competitions."

"Let's not be hasty, Alice," Jim put in. "The skin edges are pretty even. I looked at it when I changed your bandage the other day. Mr. Cavuto is practically a plastic surgeon. Your arm looks better than it did before you got shot."

"Thank you, young man," Cavuto told him. "Keep it dry for a few more days. Okay, Alice?"

"Yes," she answered, "I will, and Jim, only in your dreams would I ever enter a swimsuit competition. Tell me, though, Mr. Cavuto, what do you really think about my neighbor? Do you think your friends are going to do him any good?"

"Alice, I'd like to say they won't do

him any harm, but I can't know that for sure. Something was bound to happen on the waterfront with the big immigrations from Italy and Puerto Rico. They're even starting to call it the West Side instead of Hell's Kitchen. These people, my friends, have a certain affection for me. They bring me plenty of business, both living and dead. As that demonstrates, they are in a ferocious line of work, and they have to play the cards they're dealt. Your customs friend is one of those cards. I'd like to tell you not to worry, but I can't. He was in trouble before Manny even talked to me. Give it time. They'll try to keep him as safe as they can if only to protect the business they want to use him for. Please, don't forget your friend's recent rash behavior. He didn't do himself any favors beating up Menken's messenger."

"He knows it was stupid."

"That understood," Cavuto said, "how about you and your friends let me know how my latest tomato sauce turned out."

Roberto drained the spaghetti and

placed a generous forkful in each bowl, ladled sauce on top, and grated parmesan over each serving. He poured himself some wine and sat at the head of the table, glass in hand.

"You boys," he addressed Alice's associates. "I look at you, especially you two"—he indicated Antonio and Jotaro—"and I see that you are capable of much trouble. Don't do anything stupid. No matter how big you are physically, lead is stronger than flesh, as Miss White has just found out. And these people deal in lead. If you want to do something helpful for Mr. Applewood, see what you can do about finding his gun. The Irish must still have it. As far as your man himself is concerned, maybe we could arrange for him to get lost in the shuffle, and you won't have to do a thing, except, maybe, get him a new identity and another place to live."

# CHAPTER 22

## BENNETT

Harry was distraught. The time had come to confess his infidelity to Elaine. The intensity of his recent encounter with her at the Davises 'house had made him feel even more guilty about stepping out on her. He loved her more than he ever had, and this dishonesty would eventually erode the bond between them.

He took out a clean sheet of stationery and a fountain pen.

*Dear Elaine,*

*I cannot express to you in words how much I love you. You have been a wonderful wife to me. I am very sorry we have been unable to have children. After you read this, you may be glad we never did.*

*I have been unfaithful to you. There is no excuse for such behavior. It has been eating me alive ever since it happened. I wanted to tell you face to face, but I am too much of a coward to witness your disappointment and anger at this betrayal.*

*How can I ask you to forgive me? I love you with all my heart and, if you ever do find it in your heart to forgive me, please know that I would never do that kind of thing again.*

*If you want a divorce, I will understand. No matter how painful this is for both of us, I would never have been able to keep this a secret from you.*

*All my love,*

*Harry*

He read it over and sealed it in an envelope in care of the Davises. He'd get the address from Alice in the morning. He stamped the envelope and went to bed.

In Stanton the next morning, Milt Davis folded back his morning newspaper and bit into a slice of toast. The kitchen smelled delicious from breakfast. Sunlight streamed in through the open window. Birds chirped outside.

He put down the paper and asked, “Is this a perfect day, or what?”

Elaine had joined him and Ellen in the kitchen for breakfast. She sat at the table in a pink terry cloth bathrobe.

“You have everything you need, Elaine?” Milton asked her.

Elaine set her coffee down. “Yes, Milt. I think so. I have a new *Reader’s Digest* and a box of chocolates. What more could a girl want? I agree. This day is honestly beautiful.”

Ellen informed her, “There’s sliced baloney in the fridge and fresh rye in the bread box if you want something easy for lunch, Elaine. There's a jar of mustard on the second shelf. I'll be home early. My shift at the hospital is over at three."

Ellen was wearing her white nurse's uniform.

"Thank you both very much," Elaine told the Davises. "You've been so kind to me. I think I'll take a walk around the town square later, to get some fresh air."

"Excellent idea," Milt responded. "No one from the city knows you're up here, and I told some of the housewives I do work for that you are my cousin, here from Milwaukee. I hope you know something about Milwaukee, Elaine."

"No, I don't, Milt. What state is it in?"

"Oh, God, Milton." Ellen was exasperated with her husband. "For heaven's sake. You couldn't have picked someplace like Chicago?"

"Okay, okay. I'm sorry. Milwaukee is in, uh . . . I'll look it up before I leave. That's where they make Schlitz beer, you know, 'the beer that made Milwaukee famous. 'Geez. You girls are a tough audience."

"Honey." Ellen's mood changed. "Are you okay for lunch?"

"Don't worry about me, El," Milt answered. "Betty Mathews insists on making me lunch whenever I work in her house. I'm plumbing in a sink and a toilet next to Sam's workshop in the basement."

"Good then," Ellen responded.

She stood, washed the breakfast dishes, and put them in the rack to dry.

"I'm off." Ellen moved efficiently around the table, dispensing kisses. "You two have a great day. See you later."

With that, Ellen went over to the small mirror next to the door to the garage and pinned her starched white cap in place, grabbed the brown paper bag with her lunch in it and her purse off the counter, and exited into the garage.

Milt stood, gave Elaine a peck on the cheek, and told her, "By the way, I just remembered, as if anyone is going to ask you, Milwaukee is in Wisconsin. They might joke with you about beer. Blatz is from there too. You have a nice day." With that, he was off to the garage himself.

Elaine switched on the radio and turned the dial until she heard the comforting voice of Arthur Godfrey joking with his sidekick about his poor gardening skills.

Ten minutes later, Elaine heard *knock, knock, knock* at the house's front door.

Elaine adjusted the wrap of her bathrobe before she opened it.

A pleasant appearing heavyset man in a rumpled gray suit and a matching hat was standing there. He wasn't a bad-looking guy, a little overweight. She was curious about who he was.

He removed his hat before speaking. "Good morning, ma'am. I don't wish to alarm you, but I'm a police detective from New York City. My name is Andrew Bennett."

He showed her his badge and held it up long enough for her to carefully inspect it. Then he held out an identification card with his picture on it.

“Here are my credentials. Take them inside and lock the door. Look them over. Call my chief if you need to. His number is down at the bottom, on the front. I’ll wait out here for you to get dressed. If you decide to run out the back door, I won’t stop you. Just, please, leave my credentials somewhere I can find them. This is about the trouble your husband is in in the city. I’d like to help, but I don’t know exactly how yet. If it’s any comfort to you, I don’t think he killed that man on the waterfront.”

Elaine took the credentials from Bennett’s hand and withdrew into the house. She locked the door as he had instructed and put the chain on, looked over the picture and the written identification, decided it was probably legitimate, but called his boss anyway.

Her husband, Harry, was in way over

his head and needed whatever help he could get. Maybe there was something this detective could do to help him.

A sympathetic police officer might be of great assistance. Even so, she thought, this one could be lying about his real motivation to gain her trust. On the other hand, somehow, she believed his intentions were honorable. She decided to take a chance.

She unlocked the door and handed his credentials back to him. “Wait out here. Give me some time to get myself together.”

Bennett smiled a polite smile and told her, “Thank you, ma’am. Take all the time you need. If you don’t mind, I’ll have a cigarette out here while I wait.”

“No, I don’t mind at all,” Elaine replied. She took an ashtray off the table inside the door and handed it to him. She closed and locked the door and went to her room to get dressed.

When Elaine emerged onto the front porch in dark slacks and a white short-sleeved blouse, Detective Bennett stubbed his cigarette out in the ashtray and asked her, "Is there someplace public where we can sit and have a cup of coffee, ma'am? I make it a point never to interview a woman alone in her house. I'm divorced, but when I was married, seeing the things a police officer sees, I worried that something like that would happen to my wife, you know, the polite, fake policeman attacking her."

"How thoughtful," Elaine told him and gazed into his dark brown eyes. He made her feel safe. She felt something else too, but she was a married woman and quickly discarded the thought. Being separated from her husband was affecting her more than she had realized. What this man needed was a woman of his own to smooth out his rough edges, just not her. She could see he was exhausted, but worse, she saw a look of sadness on his face.

"There's a coffee shop a short walk from here," Elaine told him. "It's a beautiful day. I was going to take a walk myself anyway. Let me get my purse, and we can go."

She took the ashtray out of his hand and went back inside. He couldn't help but notice that she had a very nice figure. As a professional and a public servant, he compelled himself to look away.

They sat at a small table by the window in the coffee shop. Bennett had cinnamon toast with black coffee. Elaine just had coffee.

"Your husband lied to my partner, Detective Gerard, and me," Bennett told Elaine, "when we questioned him about the victim of the shooting. You don't have to talk to me about this, but I know you're both in some trouble. I followed him up from the Bronx the other night when he came here to see you. You don't hide under a blanket on the back floor of a station wagon unless you're anxious about being followed."

"Yes," Elaine answered. "He missed me." She blushed at the memory of their desperate behavior in the bedroom that night.

It was the most exciting experience she had ever had along those lines.

"I can understand." Bennett, being a detective, noticed her color and blushed himself at the thought of what must have happened in that house while he was parked outside chain-smoking and guzzling whiskey.

"The point is." Bennett quickly pulled himself together. "You and your husband are clearly in a fix, and I'd like to help, not to mention, it would go a long way to solving the murder we're investigating."

"I don't know where to begin," Elaine told him. "I don't want to get him into any more trouble than he's already in. It is true, his life and mine are in danger. That's why I'm hiding up here in Stanton. He does have a new lawyer to help him, but I'm afraid there will be no way either of you could save his job with customs, and you might even send him to jail, I think. God, I've already said too much. Maybe you should talk to Harry's lawyer; after all, that's what lawyers are for."

"That's exactly right," Bennett told her.

"Don't say another word. I need to question Harry in the presence of his attorney. I swear to you that I will do everything I can for him. I don't ever want you feeling guilty about the little you've told me. Harry is a United States Customs inspector at the Port of New York. It isn't hard to put some of this together. You wouldn't happen to know the name of Harry's attorney, would you?"

"Yes," Elaine answered him. "Clarence Eaton. He's a new member, I think, of the law firm where our neighbor, Alice White, works. It's Bryce and Adams, Attorneys at Law, on Nassau Street in Manhattan."

"That's very good," Bennett commented. "I know of Mr. Eaton. He has a reputation in my department as a straight shooter. He'll do his best to protect your husband, and, I'd bet, he will encourage him to be truthful with us. I'll call him, and he can contact Harry."

"Thank you so much. The two of us are desperate," Elaine told Bennett. "I would appreciate whatever you can do."

"No, Mrs. Applewood, thank you for talking to me. I'll walk you back to the house," Bennett told her. "I think it would be best for you to stay right here until you hear otherwise from your husband or us. Is there anything I can get for you?"

"That's very kind of you," Elaine answered, "but no, not at the moment. Just help my husband and keep him safe."

"I'll do my best, ma'am," Bennett told her, flashing his most reassuring smile.

Elaine felt something in the pit of her stomach she had not felt since the other night with Harry. She smiled back, blushed, and looked somewhere else.

Bennett noticed her embarrassment and caught his breath. She was a married woman in distress. *Shame on me*, he thought. She was a citizen of New York City whom he was sworn to protect, not take advantage of while she was separated from her husband.

He paid the bill and walked with her into the sunshine of the lovely spring day.

Al Menken finished his glass of enhanced milk and motioned for another. Louis generously spiked another milk with whiskey for his boss and, while he was at it, poured himself half a cup of whiskey and finished it with coffee. He turned up the radio so Anna would know not to disturb them.

*The bases are loaded, and Mantle is at bat*, Mel Allen announced loudly. *How do the Yankees manage to do it? It's another beautiful day for them here at Yankee Stadium, the house that Ruth built.*

"We gotta do something," Menken shouted over the sound of the game. "We're losing it. We can't just let the spaghetti-eaters walk in and take what they want."

"How is this happening?" Shaughnessy asked. He was deliberately withholding the information lovely Cindy Pinsky had provided him about Alice White's plan to take down his boss. He was positive Menken would instruct him to kill White when he found out about her. He didn't know who else was involved in screwing up Menken's operation, but it didn't take a genius to suspect that Applewood had been persuaded to cooperate with the Italians. He was the only one, besides Menken and Shaughnessy, who knew exactly which crates contained their guns. Before he took Alice White out, Louis wanted to see how things would come down for Menken. He could feel the walls closing in on his boss. This was no time to do a murder and put himself out on a limb he was sure Menken would saw off at the slightest threat to his own survival. Shaughnessy did not doubt that Menken would direct the law to his doorstep in a second to save his own skin if he were nailed for the death of Alice White.

"I don't know," Menken told him. "It's time for our friend in the police department to earn his money. Start with my nephew. Let's see if our cop can convince him to take over for Applewood and not lose his nerve. Don't have him hurt Philip if he can help it. After all, he's my sister's kid. Someone's getting to our shipments and taking a cut. Thank God it can't be my nephew 'cause he doesn't know one crate from another and, if he did, he wouldn't have the guts. My sister would kill me if I sent young Philip to a watery grave. I'm not surprised they're only taking half the shipments. They're sending us a not-so-subtle message. Applewood's gotta be in on it. Right?"

"Yeah, boss. It looks that way," Louis replied. He had to ask, "You want me to kill him?"

"No," Menken told him. "Not before I talk to him. Bring him to me. We'll torture him, maybe see if we can use him to screw with these guys. Then we'll find his wife, wherever she is, and kill them both."

Philip Madison cowered in the bushes behind the glass booth where Applewood stood talking on the phone.

"Yes. This afternoon. In from Marseilles," Harry spoke into the receiver. "I'll chalk the crates. Just make sure your men wipe the chalk off when they're done. These guys have to be getting suspicious of me. I want to live through this ordeal if at all possible."

Sarisoto kept a safe distance from Applewood. He watched the little pip-squeak, Madison, spying from the bushes. It was definitely time to get Applewood out of here to safety.

That night Sarisoto was delayed in Manhattan, conferring with Antonio. Harry was securely locked in his apartment, waiting for his protector to arrive to discuss the incredible escalation in danger that had occurred and what they should do about it. Both locks were engaged; the chain was tight and in place. He was sad but relieved that he had mailed his letter of confession to Elaine.

He hardly tasted the roasted chicken with peas he'd prepared per Elaine's instructions. The doorbell rang. *It must be Sarisoto*, he thought. Alice had told him not to open the door to anyone except his Japanese bodyguard.

"Who's there?" he spoke through the door.

"Delivery for Applewood," came a gruff voice from the hallway outside.

*That is definitely not Sarisoto. It sounds suspiciously like one of those thugs who beat me up.*

Harry was not falling for this twice. Where was his burly new Japanese friend when he needed him? Jotaro was supposed to be here.

Harry looked through the peephole and saw blackness. *It must be too dirty to see through*, he thought. It never occurred to him that someone had their hand over the other side. He pulled on the chain to make sure it was tight and secure and unlocked the two locks so he could crack the door an inch. A tremendous force from outside broke the chain and slammed the door into Harry's forehead. The same two monsters who had beaten him up were back, up close and personal. They entered the apartment.

"Don't make us hurt you any more than we have to," Pete spoke. "You're coming with us."

It was pitch black outside the basement entrance of the building.

Sarisoto walked briskly up the hill from the car he had parked on Wilbert. He spotted the two men, one of them gripping Harry's arm. His martial instincts took over.

Years of training in the frigid mountain passes of Japan came into play. He had arrived in the Bronx at the perfect moment. He walked his large frame silently into the shadow of the building and let the trio move a few paces past him down the hill he had just ascended. Pete led with Harry in his grip. Scar brought up the rear.

Jotaro stepped forward onto the ball of

his left foot, lifted his enormous right leg high in the air, into a vertical arc, and brought it straight down onto Scar's right shoulder in an ax kick, breaking Scar's collarbone and separating his shoulder at the joint. Sarisoto's foot found the ground, freeing his other to piston smoothly and powerfully into Scar's back. Scar was thrown forward, slamming his face into the pavement, rendering him unconscious. He skidded past Pete and Applewood, dropped off the curb, and came to rest under a parked truck. There he lay, breathing but unconscious.

Irish Pete turned to grab Sarisoto's ankle but could not get purchase on the enormous appendage. Jotaro dropped the leg to the ground, spun completely around backward, skipped his foot off the cement, and lifted it into a perfectly horizontal spinning back kick, practically taking Pete's head off at the neck. Pete dropped unconscious to the sidewalk. Jotaro bowed ceremonially to the two men lying quietly on the ground, then turned and grasped Harry's shoulder and began to move him down the hill.

"Where've you been?" Harry commented as they moved. "I don't mean to be ungrateful, but I was sure I was a dead man."

"Better late than never," the warrior responded. "I was downtown with Antonio discussing where to take you. It is time to get you out of here."

Jotaro conducted the dazed inspector to his parked car. Harry was developing quite a large, angry lump on his forehead.

On the street in front of his funeral home, Roberto Cavuto got behind the wheel of the gray Oldsmobile. Frankie Windows deposited the box of cannolis, which dangled from his thin fingers, onto the back seat.

They drove up the hill to the

Concourse, took a right heading south, left on Fordham Road, then over to Arthur Avenue, into the neighborhood of Enzo Trusgnich's men's club. A different kid with a shotgun greeted them inside, cradling the weapon in the crook of his arm, and knocked twice on the door to the back.

"Yeah?" came a voice from behind the door.

"Tell Mr. T. his visitors are here." He slid his hands back onto the barrel and stock of the shotgun and sat back down to wait for trouble.

A moment later, Enzo Trusgnich came through the door and motioned his two guests into the back.

Before they sat down, Roberto spoke. "Nice to see you again, my friend." He put his hands on Enzo's shoulders and kissed both his cheeks.

"It's nice to see you too, Roberto," Enzo rasped, the hint of a friendly grimace across his frozen face, his eyes softening.

Trusgnich spotted his other guest. "Frankie," he exclaimed, "it's been years. I'm honored you came down from the fire escapes to see me." His eyes shined. He managed an even broader smile, as much as the stiff muscles of his face permitted. "I thought you were retired."

Frankie's eyes twinkled, and he smiled back at Enzo. The gaps in his teeth accented his playful grin. "Yeah, Enzo. It's been too long. I haven't forgotten how much fun we used to have. Those days are over. I got too old for the excitement. At least I thought I did. All that violence wore me out, but now it found me again. No matter how peaceful I try to live, the world creeps in. I had to go to Florida to straighten something out. Then this thing on the docks. That's why we're here. Now that I know where you are, I promise I won't let so much time go by without visiting you again. Here's a little peace offering." Frankie held the string around the white cardboard box and lifted it into the air. "Cannolis."

Three glasses of anisette sat waiting on a table for the old friends.

"Salute," Enzo announced, lifting his glass into the air, and took a sip.

"Salute," the two visitors said in return. They raised their glasses.

"What can I do for you?" Enzo asked.

"Your business is none of our business, Enzo," Cavuto answered, "but we got involved with this trouble at the waterfront as I told you when we last spoke."

"Yeah, and I wash this customs guy's windows." Frankie chuckled.

"Alice White, our friend in the same building on the Concourse as Applewood, told us two Irish bruisers tried to take him away last night. I think they planned to hurt him, maybe even kill him," Cavuto commented.

Enzo Trusgnich paused before responding.

"Yeah," he finally spoke. "I sorta put him in a, what-a-ya-call-it, conflict of interest."

Frankie spoke up. "A big Japanese friend of White's took these men out, not for good, but he put them down, maybe broke one of their shoulders. He drove our guy away and hid him, probably in Manhattan. We don't know where. I don't guess he's gonna be any more use to you and your friends, huh?"

"Good," Enzo told them. "I'm glad he's safe. He's a good man. He's got a lotta nerve. I asked him where his wife was hiding—imagine me, scary old crow—and he stood up to me, wouldn't tell me where she was. I would've told me. Maybe not. Still, he reminds me of me. But business is business, and we thought maybe we'd share him with the Irish. I guess we'll have to find another way to get what we want."

"So he's straight with you?" Roberto asked.

"Yeah, sure," Enzo answered. "He did what he could. There's plenty more fish in the sea. We'll find another inspector.

"Sally," Enzo raised his voice.

The door opened, and Salvatore stuck his head in. "Yeah, Mr. T.?"

"Bring more anisette and plates for the cannolis. My friends are here from the Concourse. I might not see them again for a while. I want to have another toast before they leave."

# CHAPTER 23

## FLYBOY

"Freddie. How good of you to come," Clarence Eaton greeted his law school brother. He opened his arms and hugged Freddie Quinn. "Want some coffee?"

"I couldn't resist your invitation, Clarence. Just the mention of Alfred Menken's name set my blood to boiling. I'd love a cup."

Clarence's secretary had not left the office after showing Quinn in.

"This feisty lass, Freddie, is Laura McDonald. We'll get together and talk about what part of Ireland we're all from later,"

Eaton told his friend.

“Laura, how about you see what the partners and Alice are doing, and maybe we can all meet in the conference room? I’ll get Freddie his coffee.”

“Right, boss,” Laura replied. “Nice to meet you, Mr. Quinn.” She shook Quinn’s hand.

“You want me to sit in and take notes?” she asked Eaton.

“Good idea, and please make a copy for Jack’s secretary, Edith, if you would.”

“Sure. I’ll leave you two to chat.”

Eaton told his classmate, “Come with me, Freddie. I’ll show you around, and you can tell me how you like your coffee.”

Freddie smiled and put his index finger an inch above his thumb, indicating how much bourbon he wanted in it.

Eaton led Quinn to a break room with an industrial-sized coffee maker and a refrigerator.

When they were back in Eaton's office, and the door was closed, Eaton took out a bottle of Elijah Craig, from Quinn's home state of Kentucky. He had bought it especially for this occasion.

Eaton broke the seal and handed it to his friend. "Help yourself," he told him and lit up a Chesterfield. He motioned the pack to Freddie.

"No thanks on the smoke, Clarence. I quit a couple of years ago, but it was mighty thoughtful of you to pick me up the bourbon. How nice you found Elijah Craig here in New York City."

"Freddie, you must know by now that you can find anything you want in New York."

They sat and caught up on their families and what they themselves had been doing professionally.

"The docks are a sorry mess," Quinn told his friend. "Those men beg for work every day while their union president lives high on the hog. Menken. He's a disgrace to the labor movement. I'd love to find a way to take him down."

"Yeah, Freddie. He has had a client of mine in a difficult situation until a few days ago. Now we're being forced to hide our client away to protect him from Menken's boys, who would surely kill him if they could get their hands on him. The man has been removed to an undisclosed location, but Menken is beating the bushes trying to find him."

An hour later, they were seated in the conference room. Eaton had introduced his classmate to Jack Bryce and Rich Adams.

Alice arrived with sandwiches. She got herself a cup of coffee and sat down next to Laura McDonald.

"Alice White," Eaton spoke to Alice, "this is my Fordham Law buddy Freddie Quinn. He flew a B-17 bomber over Germany during the war, was giving those people some serious grief until they shot him down and took him prisoner. Freddie, this is our one and only legal assistant. She's going to NYU Law School at night. Maybe we'll all be in practice together sometime in the future. Meanwhile, Alice has inadvertently become our investigator, which, I must say, she manages rather well. She made it into the papers last year for solving a murder up the Hudson River in the Catskills."

Freddie Quinn stood and offered Alice his hand. They shook.

He informed her, "I do remember seeing a piece in the *Times* about your little adventure. That builder is one lucky man."

Jack Bryce cut in. "You don't know the half of it, Freddie. Even though she hated him on sight when they met and both had sworn they would live alone for the rest of their lives, they reached a tentative agreement and became a couple. It's fun watching them squirm. They're adorable together."

Alice endured the chatter about her private life with minimal embarrassment. She opened the untouched paper bag on the table and distributed turkey on rye and ham and cheese sandwiches to the group.

"There's mustard in those cardboard containers," she told them.

"Okay," Eaton announced. "I guess this is my show. I got everyone together to discuss getting our client, Harry Applewood, out of his trouble with a minimum of damage. He was, after all, coerced into his role in the smuggling operation at the port. We might not be able to save his job with customs, but you never know. We must surely try to keep him out of prison, and we need to find a way to show he didn't commit the murder he's suspected of. I'm sure Freddie would be pleased to assist if we could help the government prove Alfred Menken did it."

A block south of Luigi's, on Wilbert

Avenue, was a pool hall called Mochio's. Jim brought Alice there once in a while. They'd started playing pool their first evening out together in Stanton. She began enjoying the game with practice and was happy to discover this pool hall in her very own Bronx neighborhood.

Circles of light shone down from green conical metal fixtures hanging over each of the tables in use. Most of the hall was in darkness, even on a bright day outside. A soft light emanated from the bar, where two men sipped whiskey and smoked cigarettes, lost in conversation. A thin tattooed woman tended the bar. A ribbon of smoke drifted up from an ashtray near her cash register. Neon beer signs outlined the perimeter of the room.

Antonio Vargas sensed a climax approaching in the matter Alice White had drawn him into. He was not letting her out of his sight until the tension he felt around her subsided. Antonio sat by himself at a small table in silent contemplation. A jazz composition played low on the jukebox.

Jotaro Sarisoto strode in with a sports bag and sat down next to his friend.

"What are you doing here?" Antonio quietly asked him.

"You told me you'd be here," Jotaro answered. "I left Harry in my place downtown to come up here and get some things from his apartment for him. He asked me to get some of his T-shirts, socks, underwear, and a few books. I thought I'd drop in and see how you were doing before I head back downtown."

The bartender came over and took Jotaro's order. He asked for a beer. Antonio signaled he was okay with his water. The two men sat and watched Jim and Alice take turns shooting.

Alice sank her fourth ball in a row, off a cushion into a side pocket.

"Alice, you're killing me," Jim complained, taking a sip of his beer.

"You ought to lay off the alcohol when you play, Jim," Alice told him, smiling sweetly, lining up her next shot. "I read that in a magazine."

"I created a monster," Jim spoke back at her.

Their concern with Harry's safety was momentarily appeased, what with Harry hidden in Jotaro's apartment. They planned to smuggle him out of town to join his wife later today after the sun went down.

The fire door opened momentarily, sending in a blast of sunlight and heat, silhouetting a man passing into the room. The door closed behind him. Out of the shadows into the light of the pool table, a young man emerged in a black T-shirt with a bandana covering his lower face. He raised a gun and pulled the trigger twice.

*Blam, blam!* Both shots hit Jotaro Sarisoto in the chest.

The fire door opened again, silhouetting the gunman.

Antonio leaped at Alice, reached around behind her in a violent, almost romantic embrace, pulled her Browning from the small of her back, and shot the gunman once in the back. The man's fallen body kept the fire door from closing and left a ribbon of sunshine to penetrate the stillness of the room.

The sound of gunfire subsided.

Antonio grabbed Jotaro, slumped in his chair, held him in his arms, and slowly let him down to the floor.

"Take it easy, Jo," he told the big Japanese man. "You're gonna be okay." To the bar, Vargas shouted, "Call an ambulance!"

"No need, my friend," Jotaro whispered. "My purpose on earth is done. My karma is paid. Maybe we'll see each other down the road and have another steak sandwich at Delmonico's. Goodbye, Antonio-san."

# CHAPTER 24

## HOLED UP

Scott Gerard held his head and paced around his third-story Cherry Street walk-up. *My head is about to explode*, he thought. He'd moved to this apartment in Manhattan from the picket-fenced house on Staten Island when his wife, Ruth, died of cancer a few years ago.

He wore dungarees and a T-shirt, planning to blow off some steam at the gym when the headache subsided.

Alcohol would help. He grabbed a bottle of vodka from the refrigerator and took a long pull. His partner Andy's habits were rubbing off on him. It was clear to him that Andy was a full-blown, completely hopeless alcoholic. But these past two weeks, Scott hadn't been able to contain his depression and rage without alcohol. Something had died inside him when his wife passed away, but he was coping, until now. An unhealthy thirst for alcohol had overtaken him.

What to do about Applewood, he wondered? Harry A. was as patriotic and gutsy a man as Gerard had ever met. He admired the man. Harry had landed troops at Salerno during the Allied invasion in September 1943. *I could have been on his boat*.

While Harry, a war hero, was being beaten down by a waterfront mobster in civilian life, Scott Gerard was busy selling out the badge he held sacred to that same man. He tried not to blame it on his despair at Ruthie's death. He was hell-bent on self-destruction, and there wasn't a thing he could do to resist the pull of his wife from her grave.

*Too bad*, *Harry,* Gerard thought.

*Nothing personal, but if I have to take you down with me, and with the bad guys I work for, I will.*

He left his apartment. He entered a five-and-dime on the street, got into a phone booth, and turned the dial to connect with his clandestine employer.

"Shaughnessy," he spoke into the instrument. "Yeah, it's me. Tell your boss his escaped fish is holed up at Sarisoto's place downtown. You know, Jotaro Sarisoto, the big Japanese guy your boy just killed at the pool hall in the Bronx. Please don't bother to deny it. Here's the address."

Closer to the gym, he ducked into a mom-and-pop grocery store, used his last dime, and dialed the other of his subcontractors. He was going to give his fellow veteran, Harry Applewood, a fighting chance to survive, just barely.

"Sally," Gerard announced, "it's your favorite cop on the beat. Tell Mr. T. he doesn't have much time to save his new customs employee. He's holed up in

Manhattan. It's on Canal. Here's the address. I just got a tip that people are on the way there to kill him. Tell Enzo he'd better get a move on."

Now it was in God's hands. He washed his own of Applewood's blood.

Maybe they'd kill each other off, and Applewood would survive. He didn't know. He was approaching the end of the sick game he had begun when Ruth had left him.

On his way out of the grocery, he made the three-ring sign and asked the man for Ballantine beer, just like Broderick Crawford always said at the end of *Highway Patrol*, followed by, "The laws of your community are enforced for your protection. Obey them!" The clerk smiled and pulled a can of Ballantine beer out of his fridge.

Sarisoto's place was on Canal Street,

above a surplus electronic components store, in Lower Manhattan. It was a rainy spring morning. Harry was going bonkers, knowing his Japanese host had been killed, waiting for Alice and Jim to come and get him out of here like they promised they would on the phone. Sarisoto's place was small and dingy. He flipped through whatever newspapers and magazines he could find and listened to music over a radio with a missing tuning knob on the kitchen table. He'd gotten very little sleep. The only things left in the refrigerator were a few cans of beer and a salami. That would have to do for breakfast until his friends arrived. Maybe the beer would calm his nerves.

*Where are they?*

The clouds burst. It was now pouring outside the window.

"Use the wipers," Irish Pete told Scar. Scar was steering and shifting with his left hand. His right arm was in a sling. He took his hand off the wheel and turned on the wipers.

"That's the address, on the door next to the surplus store," Pete told him. "Pull into the space in front and leave it running."

Pete got out of the car and raised the collar of his jacket against the rain. He reached the vestibule in two strides, stairs leading to the apartments above. The wall with the mailboxes and buzzers was separated from the staircase inside a locked plate glass door. He looked at the buzzers. Only one was missing a name, #4. That had to be Sarisoto's. He pushed the button with the highest apartment number on it, then the next down. One of them buzzed him in.

Seconds later, Trusgnich's men arrived, two handsome young Italians, Ricci and Marcello. They spotted Scar behind the wheel of the running car. Marcello came up behind Scar with his silenced .45 and put a bullet through the closed window into Scar's left ear. Scar's body fell forward and added the familiar New York sound of a blaring horn to the patter of the morning's rainfall.

Ricci saw the blank nameplate on #4 and pushed a few of the other buttons until someone buzzed him in. Just before the door closed behind him, Marcello slid in. They quickly ascended the stairs in tandem.

Irish Pete kicked with all the force of his massive frame into the wooden door of apartment #4. It splintered inward under his boot. He raised his gun and found his shocked target cowering on the far side of a wooden dining table. Before he could get a shot off, *pfft*, a silenced bullet tore through his back, collapsing his right lung, dropping him to a knee, forcing him to drop his gun. He gasped short breaths. He reached down and recovered the gun with his left hand. Without turning around to face his attacker, he pointed it over his shoulder and placed a single shot in Ricci's forehead, swiveled, and shot Harry Applewood twice, once in the throat, once in the chest. Marcello, seeing his partner fall dead, finished Irish Pete with two shots to the base of his skull and took off down the stairs, two at a time.

As Harry lay dying, he thought about his beautiful wife, Elaine, and the letter he had sent her confessing his sins. Maybe it would soften the blow of his passing.

Minutes later, Jim Peters drove up outside Sarisoto's building. Jim, Alice, and Antonio followed the car horn's noise to the body draped over the still-running car's steering wheel.

# CHAPTER 25

## COPS

"It was an accident waiting to happen," Gerard told his partner, hiding his guilt and shame.

Bennett sat behind the wheel of their department car, finishing a cigarette. They were parked in front of Murphy's Bar.

"Maybe," Bennett responded, "but I still think there was something we coulda done to keep Applewood alive."

He lowered his window to let some of the smoke out.

Bennett felt terrible about the loss of life but, more importantly, worse about the horrible pain it had inflicted on Applewood's widow. They were people too decent to get mixed up in a nightmare like this.

"Don't lose any sleep over it," Gerard told his partner. "Applewood got himself in with the wrong people, is all."

The detectives were there to question Murphy about the multiple deaths, since two of them were his regulars. They had driven over from the customs house, where they had interviewed Applewood's colleague, Philip Madison. Nothing there, although, interestingly, Madison had reacted to the news of his coworker's demise with fear, not sadness.

Harry had been shot. Three other dead bodies had been found: two waterfront thugs and one recent immigrant from Italy, a mob hoodlum, no doubt. There was not much hope that anyone would have anything enlightening to say about what had happened, but they had to ask.

The car's ashtray was full. Bennett tossed his cigarette out the window.

Inside, Murphy was drying glasses, as though he had not stopped since they spoke to him the week before. A fountain of information he was not.

"Nah," Murphy replied to Gerard, "I have no idea what happened there. I know I lost two good customers, and it's a crying shame."

"Yeah, well," Gerard commented.

Gerard turned to his clearly unhappy partner and surprised him by asking, "Want one for the road?"

Bennett's eyebrows went up. What had happened to Gerard's strict prohibition against alcohol on the job? "No thanks," he replied, "but you go ahead without me."

"Whiskey," Gerard told the owner. "Make it a double . . . and a beer."

Bennett took in his partner's strange behavior with a cold chill. The rock had cracked. This was not good. Something was seriously eating the man. Gerard hadn't had much of a private life since his wife died. But this was different. Something about this case they were working on was clearly getting to him. Bennett almost didn't want to know what it was.

After leaving Murphy's establishment, Bennett flipped Gerard the keys to their car.

"I'll catch the train to the station house. I need some time to walk," Andy told his partner and headed off on foot.

Andy Bennett went over to a church on John Street. He took the steps down to the basement, found the community room, and took a seat in the back. Cigarette smoke filled the air. Most people had a cup of coffee in their hands. After the preliminaries and someone had asked if anyone wanted to speak, Andy spoke up. "Hi, everyone. My name is Andy, and I am an alcoholic."

Elaine Applewood returned to the Davises 'breakfast table from their bathroom.

Ellen Davis asked her, "Aren't you feeling any better? You've been sick a few days now."

"Yes, it is hanging on, but I'll be okay," Elaine answered her. "It's just a stomach bug."

Milton Davis turned to his wife, Ellen, and rolled his eyes toward the ceiling. They had two children.

"Elaine," Ellen tentatively offered, "if you don't mind me asking a personal question, how do your breasts feel?"

"It's funny you ask. I think, from all this retching, I must have strained something," Elaine answered her. "They're pretty sore."

"Elaine," Milt interjected. "Have you given any thought to the possibility that you might be pregnant? It is just a possibility. These things happen. They happened to Ellen and me, uh, twice."

"Do you think?" Elaine mused. "We haven't ever been able to conceive, you know. We sort of gave up on the idea of being parents. We've been perfectly happy without children. Harry's gonna flip if it turns out I'm pregnant. Oh my God, Ellen. Do you think it's possible?"

"I can't say for sure without a pregnancy test, Elaine, but you and Harry didn't exactly keep it quiet the night he visited you here."

Elaine blushed deeply, remembering her and her husband's shameless behavior. "Gee, I'm sorry, we didn't mean to carry on so audibly. That's never happened before."

"I rest my case," Ellen concluded. "Don't apologize. We were very happy for you, but, I'd say, a torrent of withheld passion in a strange environment would be just the thing to lower your resistance to getting pregnant. Why don't you come down to the hospital later, and I'll have one of the doctors order you a test. It's very early for these symptoms to occur, but it's been known to happen."

"Oh, my," Elaine exclaimed. "Oh, my."

"Yep," Milt commented. "That just about covers the subject."

They sat quietly, each lost in their own worlds: Elaine considering the possibility of motherhood, Milton and Ellen remembering their years of raising children.

*Ring. Ring.* The telephone startled them all.

Ellen picked it up. "Hello."

Her face fell. "Yes, Alice. I'll put her on."

Ellen handed her guest the telephone. Tears flooded her eyes.

Elaine saw the shock on Ellen's face and became very still. Hesitantly, she reached for the receiver and put it to her ear.

After a while, Elaine's sobbing turned into guttural cries of grief.

She handed the phone back to Ellen.

“Yes,” Ellen spoke into the instrument. “Yes, all right, Alice. I’ll call in sick today. She’s welcome to stay with Milt and me for as long as she wants.”

Later that morning, after Milt had left for the job he was working on, the phone rang again.

“Hello,” Ellen answered. “Yes, she’s here. Can I ask who’s calling? Yes, okay. I’ll see if she’s up to speaking with you.”

Ellen turned to her grieving guest. “It’s a police detective. Are you up to speaking to him? He says his name is Andrew Bennett.”

“Yes, of course,” Elaine answered. “He’s the detective I told you about who took me out for coffee.

“Hello, Detective Bennett.”

She listened. “No, it was not your fault. We knew the odds were against either of us surviving from the very beginning. There was always the chance that one or both of us would be killed. You just walked into the middle of it and did the best you could to help. Harry and I were very grateful. Thank you and your partner for giving Harry the benefit of the doubt. He told me he should have involved the authorities long before you questioned him, and I guess he paid the price."

Pause. "What's that? Yes, I know you'll do everything you can to find out who's responsible. Yes, when I'm ready, I'd like that very much. It's very nice of you to offer. You must be awfully busy. You don't have to do that. Yes, okay, give me your number. I'll call you when I'm ready to come back to the city."

Ellen handed her a pad and pencil.

"Yes. I have it. Thank you," she said, and she hung up.

"He says I should call him when I'm ready, and he'll pick me up and take me," Elaine told Ellen. "They're obviously going to do what they can to find out who sent the men to kill Harry, but I'm not counting on anything, and, really, does it even matter now?"

That afternoon the letter from Harry arrived.

"I'm pregnant," Elaine blurted out once her things were in the trunk of Andy Bennett's car and they were on the parkway driving south toward the Bronx. "Can you even believe it? And Harry's not even alive to appreciate this miracle. Gosh, I'm so sorry. I didn't mean to unburden myself on you like that. Please don't be upset because of me. I am not some pathetic widow."

Andy kept quiet. He didn't want to lie. It depressed him intensely. The baby would never know its father. He or she would be a constant reminder to Elaine of her husband and a happier time in her life that she would never get back.

Maybe the birth would give Elaine some measure of peace, a new life, a part of Harry.

No matter. Andy could not think of anything to say that would make Elaine's tragic circumstances any easier to bear, so he said nothing.

They remained quiet on the way south. The trees and the grass had been washed clean by the recent succession of rainfall. Andy lowered his window; the smell of grass and flowers poured into the car. The sky was almost cloudless. It was a weekday. Traffic would be light until they got near the city.

There was a parking space in front of Elaine's dirty white brick apartment building. Andy carried her luggage to the elevator.

"Why don't I wait for you, and I'll walk you to the grocery store after you figure out what you need?" he offered. "I can carry the food home for you, and then I'll go back to work and leave you to get settled in."

"That would be nice. Thank you. I

really don't want to impose on you."

"No trouble at all," Andy told her. "I took most of the day off. My partner is fine without me. I'll catch up with him later and see where we stand."

Andy emptied his arms of grocery bags onto Elaine's kitchen counter.

"Thanks so much for your kind help moving me back here," Elaine told him. "I didn't mean to bother you with my troubles. Thank you for what you and your partner are doing to solve Harry's murder. Considering the type of animals Harry was dealing with, there doesn't seem much hope you'll ever find out who was responsible and, if you do, be able to prove it. Harry saw this coming. He was never going to be able to walk away from them. Nothing is going to bring him back. Anyway, I have more immediate things to worry about, like raising a child without him."

"Elaine," Bennett told her before he left, "I'd like to look in on you and the baby from time to time, be a big brother if you don't mind. I could never take the place of a birth father. My wife and I never had kids of our own, but I'd like to help."

"That's so very nice of you," Elaine replied. "I can't tell you how good that makes me feel. I think you'd make an excellent male influence on a child. I'd like that very much. Please do stay in touch."

Andy smiled. "Okay then, I'll leave you to it."

# CHAPTER 26

## CHAIN OF COMMAND

Bennett picked Alice and Elaine up in the Bronx and drove them across the Willis Avenue Bridge to Alice's law firm on Nassau Street in Manhattan. It was a warm spring day. Alice rode in the back and cranked the triangular vent open for a breeze.

"What's happening with your job, Elaine?" Alice asked her neighbor.

"My boss is very generous, Alice. He told me I should take as much time as I need to put Harry's affairs in order. He graciously told me there would never be anyone to take my place and that he would limp along with an agency temp until I come back."

"That's nice of him," Bennett told her. "You must be good at your job."

"I've been with him for years. I know what he needs. I know his wife, and, uh . . ." Elaine teared up and sobbed quietly.

"What's wrong?" Alice asked her.

"Nothing," Elaine answered. "They were just over for dinner. We had a wonderful time together. Harry always got along so well with my boss. They talked about playing golf together. We had whiskey sours Harry made in an old malted machine we have in the kitchen, and Harry set out cigarettes in one of those plastic dispensers that deliver up one at a time on a cradle. You know the ones. A cigarette fell out of the ashtray and burned the leather top of Harry's desk. When our child is old enough and has a home of their own, I'm going to give them that desk to remember their father by. It's just all so new. Harry's gone. A child is on the way. A future alone. I'll be okay. I swear I will be. I have to be."

Alice reached forward from the back seat, put her hand on Elaine's shoulder, and felt her sorrow.

From his time on the job, Bennett was adept at navigating through Manhattan. He slid down side streets and weaved in and out of traffic like a race car driver. They arrived at Alice's office faster than she could believe.

Freddie Quinn and Clarence Eaton met their late client's widow and her retinue in the conference room.

"It's nice to see the police department is in attendance," Eaton told Bennett. They had spoken briefly when Harry was still alive. "Maybe we can sort this out, so the man who's responsible for Harry's death gets what's coming to him."

Elaine offered, "After you all got involved with our troubles, Harry told me more about his problem at work. It was obvious to Harry that his instructions were coming from the union president, Alfred

Menken. That young man who was killed was the first to come to Harry and threaten to have him and me hurt and even killed unless Harry approved cargo coming into the port without inspecting it. Harry was forced to accept payment for his service to keep him from blowing the whistle on them. From what Harry told me, he never had any direct contact with Mr. Menken."

"Not surprising," Quinn commented. "I've been following Menken and his organization for years to see if there was any way I could improve conditions on the docks. I would have been disappointed if Menken had not used intermediaries. We're gonna have to find a way to get to Menken through his chain of command. He has to be responsible for Harry's murder and that of the young man they were planning to frame Harry for."

He asked, "Alice? Do you have any ideas?"

Alice responded, "Harry's associate, Phil Madison, is definitely the weak link in

Menken's operation. I met him at Harry's office. The three of us went out to dinner together, and I blinded him with the charm my mother always accuses me of having. I think he took a fancy to me. Maybe I could agitate him in a way that suits our purpose. I figure he's the one who stole the gun from Harry's desk that they, no doubt, used to kill Mr. Teleducci. Maybe I could tell him that the police are looking into the possibility that whoever stole Harry's gun used it to do the murder. It seems to me that, with their main customs man gone, Madison is next in line for his job. He's gotta be getting nervous, and my guess is he's not going to be too hard to push over the edge."

NYPD Detective Scott Gerard found Phil Madison at his desk.

"Hello, Philip," Gerard greeted the young man.

"It's you. You're one of the cops that came to see me after Harry got killed," Madison said warily. "Where's your partner?"

"I'm here alone, in an unofficial capacity, sort of as a career adviser," Gerard told him.

"I don't need any advice about my career, thanks. I've been making my own career decisions for quite a while now, and I think I can get along without any outside help."

"That's where you're wrong, old boy."

"Really? What makes you such an expert?"

"I specialize in health issues in the workplace."

"Well, in that case, I really don't need your help. My health is just fine."

"Exactly," Gerard came back. "Up to now, you haven't needed my assistance, but you do now. Since your supervisor died, you're up for a promotion to his position."

"Yeah, so how is that any of your

business?" Madison asked. "In fact, if it is any of your business, I'm thinking of declining that promotion and moving out to the West Coast."

"Ya see," Gerard responded, "that's just the kind of thing your family's been worried about. They need you here, at least for now. That's where my expertise in health comes in handy."

"Wait a minute, mister. I don't owe my family anything. I have always done whatever they asked me, but now I got other fish to fry."

"That's not how they see it," Gerard told him. "They think you do owe them something. You helped them get rid of Irving T. and pin it on Harry. That sort of ties you to them for the rest of your life. There's no statute of limitation on murder or accessory to murder. They want to keep you close so they can look after your best interests. Sort of preemptive health maintenance."

*Crap,* thought Madison. *This nightmare will never end.*

"I hear you."

"Good. I knew you would. Someone will be around with further instructions. In the meantime, relax, take it easy, keep your mouth shut. Do what you're told, and everything will be just fine. It was nice meeting you."

"Likewise, I'm sure."

Alice wore a trench coat and a floppy brimmed hat as she navigated the docks. She felt the comforting presence of one of Antonio's men behind her.

"You ready for lunch?" she asked young Philip when he opened the office door.

"You are a sight for sore eyes, Alice." Madison smiled at her. "Just what I needed to take my mind off my troubles."

"New responsibilities, huh?" Alice asked him. "Don't let it get you down. Thanks for letting me buy your lunch. I was gonna be around here anyway, and I thought how nice it would be to drop in on you. I didn't know if you'd have time."

"I always have time for a beautiful woman," Madison told her. He was not feeling as free and easy as when they had dined with his late partner. As casually as he could manage, he asked, "Uh, do you know how it's going with the investigation into Harry's death?"

Could she have led him into this conversation any more smoothly than he had led himself? She thought not.

"The police say it's going slow," Alice responded. "They're fixated on the fight Harry had with the young man, Teleducci. They are desperate to find Harry's gun. It wasn't among his things at home or in his office desk here, either. They think whoever took it killed Teleducci. Can you think of who could've taken it?"

A wave of cold sweat broke out over Madison's brow. He wiped his upper lip with the side of his index finger.

"That's very interesting, Alice,"

Madison responded. "Let's head out. I have a ship to inspect this afternoon."

After lunch at a local diner, Madison escorted Alice to the subway station and practically crashed into her bodyguard when he turned to head back toward the port.

He entered his office to prepare for his first illegal act as a United States Customs inspector, the clearance of cargo on the *Baron of Barcelona*, contraband overlaid with a shipment of textiles.

Now that Harry Applewood was dead, Madison had hoped his Uncle Al would dispose of Harry's gun so his part in the murder of Teleducci would be off the table. Philip was sure his fingerprints were on the weapon along with Harry's. Now he knew, with nauseating certainty, that his uncle would never part with it, would use it to insure his loyalty. He was about to seal his fate by becoming an active participant in his Uncle Alfred Menken's criminal operation.

When Madison got back to his office from inspecting the Spanish ship, he was greeted by a cloud of cigarette smoke and a young, clearly Italian, hood sitting at his desk with his feet up. The visitor's hat was on the coat tree in the corner.

The fellow dropped his cigarette on the floor, took his feet off the desk, and stood to shake Madison's hand while he twisted out the burning ember with the sole of his shoe.

"Pasquale Mazetti; I represent the late Inspector Applewood's silent partner from the south of Italy."

Madison recognized the accent. "What now?" he asked the young immigrant.

The question did not require an answer, and it got none. Philip knew what the man was there for.

"Listen to me, Mr. Mazetti; I'm taking over this part of my family's business. Your deal with my predecessor is over."

"I don't think so," Mazetti told him.

"You stole Harry's gun and killed that guy. The people who sent me want some cooperation here, or you're going down for it. This is not just a Mick waterfront anymore. We Italians live here too, if you didn't notice. It's a new world, just like they told us it would be when we left home. You gotta give us some respect. Tell your uncle we'll settle for either a piece of the action or a bloodbath. Doesn't matter which to us. It's only right. Your guys killed one of our guys when they took out the inspector. We don't forget." Mazetti tapped his temple with a finger and stared coldly at Madison.

*Shit,* thought Madison. *This is quickly becoming worse than my worst nightmare.*

"Tell me what you want me to do?" Madison said to the stranger.

Andy had lost time from work, seeing

to Elaine. It was time to check in with his partner and get back to earning a living.

"Hey, Scott. How's it going? What you been doing while I was moving Mrs. Applewood back to the city?"

"Hello, Andy. There's nothing much going on since her husband was killed. I took another run at his coworker, Philip Madison, but no dice. He may have taken Harry's gun and passed it on to Menken, but the weapon's gone, and he's not liable to confess to anything."

"Did you ID the man who killed Harry?"

"Yeah," Scott answered. "The guy's name was Irish Pete. Everybody on the waterfront knew him. I flashed a picture of the corpse at a few of the dockworkers. His sidekick, a guy named Scar, was the one in the car outside. Then there's the Italian guy from Naples. His name was Ricci Costa."

"A lot of good any of that does us," Bennett responded to the information.

Gerard's voice was thick. Andy recognized the sound of his own speech when he had a skinful. Something bad was happening with his partner. He couldn't shake the feeling that the worst was yet to come. His partner was depressed, true, but something new had been added to his stress.

On the Upper East Side of Manhattan, on 57th Street, removed from the Port of New York docks, in the back booth of an Irish restaurant and pub, sat Alfred Menken's right-hand man, Louis Shaughnessy, reading a newspaper, smoking a cigarette, and nursing a beer. He was uncomfortable sitting there, waiting for someone. Usually, he waited for no man. Men waited for him. It was humiliating, but he had no choice. Time had run out. His face felt clammy and cold. He tried to breathe easy, to look calm, to preserve some dignity.

Detective Andy Bennett slid into the booth opposite Shaughnessy. He ordered a glass of water. He looked into the eyes of the union executive but said nothing, letting the man's own imagination do the work of persuasion for him. Bennett's years on the job had conditioned him to savor the final glide into his prey. This was not the time to trigger fear, hostility, or flight. Those emotions would only make his job more tedious. He held all the cards. He would treat Shaughnessy with respect he did not deserve, for the unpleasant job he was about to be forced to do. Louis was going to cut his boss's throat.

"You're gonna have to leave town, and I mean now," Bennett told him. "I made the arrangements. You can't even go back to your place. A car is on its way. It'll be here in the next few minutes. Just get in."

"Ironic, isn't it," Shaughnessy mused. "I suppose I always knew this day would come. Speaking of irony, I'll throw in a bonus on the house. Your partner. Just make sure he doesn't find out where you're keeping me, or I'm a dead man."

Andy's heart sank.

Scott Gerard sat on his living room couch, a lit cigarette in his mouth. Smoking was bad for his health. It was too late to worry about that now. He sat in the quiet, his mind blessedly silent for a moment.

The moment passed.

He'd always believed there was a line he would never cross, but with Applewood, he had crossed it. The man had served his country, saved other men in the war. There he was, an innocent bystander, and Gerard got him killed. He should have protected him. If their situations were reversed, Scott did not doubt that Applewood would have died protecting him. Instead, Scott had taken money from the Irish and the Italians and used his position of authority as a police officer to profit at the cost of innocent lives. That was not who he was, not why he had become a cop. He had become part of the problem instead of the solution. If he had come across a fellow officer who had done what he had just done, he would have killed him. The loss of his wife, Ruth, had hammered the nail into the coffin of his self-respect, but she was not to blame. He would not lay it at her feet. Through the rough going after the war, she had stood by him as the terror of combat gradually subsided and made it possible for him to become a respected police officer, then a detective.

Even more tragic than killing a war hero was the realization that he had widowed a hero's wife. He had condemned her to the same pathetic existence he had endured since Ruthie's death, sentenced her to that same bitter melancholy. What a despicable human being he had become.

The pride he'd once felt in the New York City Police Department was gone. They were his family, and he had turned his back on them. Would he ever forgive himself? Certainly not in this lifetime.

*I'm done,* thought Gerard with a sigh.

He stood up and took an empty glass from a kitchen cabinet. He had bought a fifth of whiskey on his way home and now he slid it out of its brown paper bag. He turned on the TV and adjusted the rabbit ears to cut the snow obscuring Henry Fonda and Harry Morgan, who were slowly riding toward the camera talking to each other. He sat down hard on his torn couch and broke the seal on the whiskey. *The Ox-Bow Incident* was maybe the most depressing movie he had ever seen. It was perfect for him to watch at this time of self-pity. He'd seen it a million times. He thought how sad it was when the skinny old colored guy sang "Lonesome Valley." He filled his tumbler and swallowed half of it in a few gulps, felt the burn, then the flush, then heard himself sigh. He finished the glass, poured himself another, and repeated the process.

Tears came to his eyes. He could still make out the hushed voices of Fonda and Morgan conversing on the screen. The idle talk, the Old West, horses snorting, all failed to connect with him. He could relate to the movie because three innocent men were about to be hanged for something they didn't do, which reminded him of what he had just done to Applewood.

Scott was having trouble getting air. He tried to take a deep breath, but his throat and chest ached and prevented him. He was in a pit of despair deeper than he ever remembered experiencing. He couldn't even stand up. He couldn't lift his arms. Futility and heartache settled on him like a lead blanket. He was never getting off this couch again. He was certain of that. The pain was just too much. It was not worth the effort.

He rolled to his left where his service weapon lay on the end table, watched his right arm swing across his chest as if moved by somebody else. The gun was in his hand, the slide pulled back, the muzzle in his mouth. The trigger squeezed itself.

# CHAPTER 27

## GIRLS' LUNCH OUT

Halfway down the hill to the Italian neighborhood behind Alice's building was a sandwich shop.

Alice opened her mouth wide and stuffed one end of a baloney on Italian bread in. Her first few chomps required a certain force and determination to break the hard crust, visibly reflected in her jaw muscles' bulge. She sucked up some Coca-Cola through a straw to wash it down. The first bite took the edge off her appetite. She caught her breath and was almost ready to engage in conversation. Elaine had a tuna on white from which she daintily bit a piece while waiting for Alice to regain her composure.

"I asked you to have lunch with me, Alice, to thank you for your kindness during this terrible ordeal. You reached out to me when no one else did."

"Are you kidding, Elaine? You would have done the same for me. Please don't thank me. Harry is dead. Could things have gone any worse?"

"Don't blame yourself. If you hadn't gotten involved, I would have had to live through this alone. I could easily have been killed as well. Harry was grateful to you for getting me out of town. Now I'm going to have his baby. That's two of us you saved."

"The Davises told me you were pregnant, Elaine. I can't imagine how you must feel about that."

"That's just it, Alice. It's sad, yes, but it's also wonderful. We were never able to get me pregnant. Now there'll be someone to remember Harry by and who will remember him after I'm gone."

"Elaine, you are a special person to be able to see it that way."

"Then, also, Alice, I'm embarrassed to mention this to you, there's this whole new issue I feel guilty about. Harry has only just died, and there's a man I'm seriously attracted to. Can you understand how disloyal I feel, Alice? I'm so ashamed."

"Who on earth is it, if you don't mind me asking?"

"I felt it when he came up to see me in Stanton, the police detective, Andy. I was ashamed even then, but I couldn't help myself. I had a physical reaction to him. I think he felt it too. He was too much of a gentleman to do anything but look away. I was a married woman. I was mortified. Then, to top that off, I found out I was pregnant at almost the same moment that Harry died."

"Don't look a gift horse in the mouth. It looks like you were not meant to suffer alone."

"Andy says he wants to help me with

the child. I already have improper feelings toward him. Oh, Alice, I really don't know what to do. He's smitten with me. No matter how he tries to hide it, I can tell. It feels so wrong."

"Elaine, there's no accounting for these things. They happen. They happened to Jim and me. We hated each other when we met. Well, at least I hated him. I think he was a goner as soon as he laid eyes on me. What can I say? I'm just so overwhelmingly beautiful. It was like shooting fish in a barrel. To top it off, we had each sworn we would never get close to another human being for the rest of our lives."

"There's one more thing I have to tell you about, Alice. In a way, it relieves some of my guilt about Andy and me."

"I don't want to impose on your privacy, Elaine. If it's too personal, don't tell me. I'll understand."

"Alice, I have to tell someone, or I'll explode."

"Okay, spill it."

"Alice, Harry had an affair. He wrote me a letter. I got it at the Davises 'after he died. He said he was too guilty to tell me in person. Alice, he cheated on me. I can't believe it. Would I have ever forgiven him? I don't know. I think I would have. I do now. I'm a mess. I'm so grateful I have you to talk to about it. You were married, now you're not. I'm sorry. I don't want to bother you with my troubles. I'm sure you and Jim have problems of your own, right?"

"Not exactly like yours, Elaine, at least I hope not, but, yes, we have issues. I think he's being very patient, waiting for me to say I'll marry him. I've got guilt of my own to deal with. He is such a wonderful man, loving like a child, strong like an ox, smart like a . . . something, loyal like a puppy. Ugh. I can't stand myself for doing this to him, but the truth is, I may never be ready for marriage again. I told myself I would never remarry. Did you know that my husband for almost a year was also a police officer, named Andy too? What turmoil we went through. Now Jim is paying for it. It isn't fair to him, but I want to be true to myself. I'm honestly not ready to commit that way."

"Oh, Alice, I love having you in my life. No matter what you do, please don't lose touch with me."

"I'm glad you trust me enough to tell me something so personal, Elaine, but I would suggest that you do not let this lapse in Harry's judgment overshadow the good memories you have of your life together. Your secret is safe with me. That said, Elaine, you know, we are girls after all, so as long as you're confiding in me, do you have any idea who it was Harry cheated on you with?"

"Gee, Alice, everything happened so fast, I haven't given it much thought. You think it's someone I know?"

"I don't know, Elaine. It just piques my imagination."

"Alice. You don't think it was Brenda, do you? Oh, God. Maybe it was. She's had her eye on him for a long time. She always says she 'just loves a man in uniform. 'I'm not even mad if it was her. I only hope she was good to him. You think I ought to ask her?"

"That's a good question, Elaine. If you're really not mad at her, I think you should leave it alone. If it was Brenda, it's going to eat at her until she can't stand it anymore, and then you can expect her to break down and confess to you. In the meantime, it'll be entertaining watching her squirm."

"Alice, you are so bad. If it was Brenda, it's gonna torture her."

"Yeah, I expect it will. That'll go a long way to helping you forgive her."

"God, Alice, I almost forgot to tell you. Andy's partner, Scott Gerard, shot himself last night. He's dead. Andy says Scott hasn't been right since his wife died a few years ago.

"Alice, I think something is going on. Arrests are going to be made, and they'll find out what happened to Harry. Andy can't tell me any of the details, but he wants me to know they won't rest until someone is held accountable."

# CHAPTER 28

## ALMOST A HIT

Philip called Harry Applewood's home phone number and got his widow on the line.

"Hello, Mrs. Applewood. My name is Philip Madison. I worked with your husband."

"Yes, Mr. Madison. Harry told me you were working with him at customs."

"I want to offer you my sincere condolences. I'm sorry for your loss."

"Thank you very much. It is so nice of you to take the time to call me."

"You are very welcome. I wonder if you could give me your neighbor's phone number. Alice White. The three of us had dinner together while you were out of town, and I have some things I want to discuss with her."

"Why certainly, Mr. Madison."

"Hello, Alice. This is Phil Madison, from the docks."

"Hi, Philip. What can I do for you?"

"Alice, I'm in big trouble, the kind of trouble your friend Harry was in before he died. This is not gonna end well for me. I took a chance calling you. If my Uncle Alfred finds out, he might even have me killed too. His right-hand man, Louis Shaughnessy, is gone, disappeared. If he talks to the police, he could blame me for everything that happened to Harry. It's not true. I didn't do anything. They made me steal his gun. You gotta help me. I need protection. I need legal advice. I need help staying alive."

"Calm down, Philip. We'll talk. I can't guarantee I can help you after what your family did to Harry. So Alfred Menken is your uncle. That's very interesting. There's a lawyer I know who's concerned about the situation on the docks. He's been looking into corruption in your uncle's union for a long time. He is quite disturbed by what he's discovered. Maybe you could make a deal with him—information for representation. I don't know. What do you think?"

"Not on the phone, Alice, but, yes, I think we can work something out. I'll tell you all about it when we meet. Where and when?"

Antonio Vargas wore a watch cap, a peacoat, his trademark black jeans, motorcycle boots, and a diver's watch. The cap was pulled over his brow. Men on the docks increased their pace as they walked past him. Certainly, no one slowed or stopped for a cigarette anywhere in his vicinity. He liked being big.

Antonio was either Mexican, Colombian, or Cuban. Nobody knew, and nobody cared. The female head of a criminal empire had taken him under her wing in his youth. She had polished his social skills and taught him the art of seduction and performance with women, taking advantage of his size and strength to satisfy her own physical needs, but careful not to fall in love with him herself. She had sent Antonio to prison for five years on behalf of a powerful man who rewarded Antonio by setting him up in a lucrative security business serving upscale restaurants and nightclubs in Manhattan. One night a year ago, Alice White had saved his life and the lives of some of his employees during the robbery of a car rental agency. No matter that he had a policy of professional detachment or that he was now married to a hot-blooded Hispanic woman of his own, Vargas recognized a lifelong debt to Alice, which he would never be able to repay.

Louis Shaughnessy had disappeared off the face of the earth, secreted away in protective custody, no doubt, by New York's finest.

Phil Madison figured, no matter where

Shaughnessy had gone, he was next in line to disappear, and so he waited nervously for Alice at the time and place she had chosen. The time was now, and the place, at the U.S. Customs House of the Port of New York.

Antonio watched the customs house from the shadows across the street. He could see through the window the profile of the little punk, Madison, squirming in contemplation of his impending betrayal of Uncle Al, which would seal his fate for life or death. Who could tell? Vargas was hoping Philip would be attacked before Alice got there. He would delay his assistance and watch the weasel be beaten, shot, or stabbed to death. Protecting Madison went against every instinct Antonio had, but Alice owned his loyalty and wanted Madison kept alive. So, he guessed, he would protect Madison with his own life. Madison's family had killed Antonio's beloved friend Jotaro. It broke Vargas's heart that he was there to protect this piece of human garbage who had gotten two good men, Jotaro and

Harry, killed. Including the bookkeeper, that made three murders, and Madison should be made to pay alongside his uncle. Instead, Philip was going to be a witness against Al Menken, and Uncle Al was either going to fry in the electric chair or be tortured and beaten to death in prison by Antonio and Jotaro's friends.

Ah, there he was, emerging from the alley, just the person Antonio was expecting. The hitman. Only he was a she. It was Vilma Pelk, the strange dockside vagrant, crawling out from the rock she had been hiding under, emerging as the ruthless killer everyone suspected she had been in her youth. Obviously, she still was. He guessed there was no retirement plan in her line of work. She wore a moth-eaten coat and a beat-up brimmed hat and stood dead still with her hands in her pockets. *Might as well wear a sign, Killer for Hire,* Antonio thought.

Oh God, did Antonio want to pretend he didn't see her and let Madison die. But Alice had him under her thumb. He briefly lost himself in musings of Miss White.

Time to stop thinking of the woman and do something about the situation unfolding in front of him before it was too late.

Antonio grabbed a rock from the ground in each hand and stuffed them into the pockets of his peacoat. He moved rapidly to Pelk's back, grabbed the would-be assassin by her lapels, and pulled her coat down over her arms, rendering her momentarily helpless. Then, swiftly and mercifully, he hammered one of the rocks with murderous force into her temple, heard her skull crack, and felt her body go lifeless in his arms. He slid a hand into her coat pocket and came up with a gun, which he threw into the harbor. He replaced it with a rock and put the second rock into her other pocket. He clutched the body and bent down for more rocks for her pockets, then lifted his package to the edge of the pier and let it slide out of his grip into the water. He stood coolly by and watched the remains of Vilma Pelk disappear under the surface.

Vargas gazed out over the water. He was glad his thoughts of Alice White had passed. After all, he belonged to another woman.

Heading toward him, down the pier, strode the seductive female investigator herself, in a trench coat and a comical oversized hat drooping down over her face. Vargas smiled and turned sideways to track her out of the corner of his eye until she was safely inside the customs house for her meeting.

He looked down at the water again to where Vilma Pelk had gone under, to assure himself she had not resurfaced.

# CHAPTER 29

## WINDOWS

Alice heard the doorbell. Frankie the window washer's face smiled its impish grin at her through the peephole, his watery eyes twinkling, the gray skullcap in place, his gray vest open. She was comforted by the familiarity of the sight, despite the pain of Harry Applewood's death and the persistent ache of her arm where the bullet had passed through. She had stuck her nose into her neighbor's business, and now he was dead. It wasn't her fault, she knew, but she needed to be consoled anyway. She opened the door.

"I'm so glad to see you, Frankie." Alice hugged the thin old man.

"Alice, what're you so glad about?" Frankie asked her. "We messed up."

"It wasn't your fault. It's not my fault either," she told him. "We did what we could. At least we saved Harry's wife, and now his child too."

"Thanks. I feel better talking to you too," Frankie told her. "Believe it or not, I'm here to do your windows. This may not be my first line of work, but it keeps me off the streets. I promise I won't jump off your fire escape again."

After washing Alice's windows, Frankie popped down the hill to Cavuto's as he had promised his friend Roberto he would.

The window washer sat at the end of Roberto's kitchen table. After years as the central platform of Cavuto family life, the surface was deeply scarred. Appliances had been repaired on it, shelves had been built on it, small children had danced on it, guns had been slammed into its surface to dramatize strong opinions during late-night business meetings. A glass of wine sat on it in front of

Frankie.

Roberto stood at the stove, sautéing onions with garlic, oregano, basil, and sausage. The aroma was almost more than Frankie could take. He was hungry.

"Hey, Frankie," Cavuto commented, "we didn't do such a good job protecting Miss White's neighbor. You think she'll ever speak to us again?"

"Ahh, don't sell her short, Roberto. I washed her windows before I came down here. We talked about it. She understands this kind of thing better than you think. The customs guy was in a bad place to start with. We tried to help him out. She reminded me at least the wife lived through it, and she's pregnant with his baby. So his kid is gonna live too. The labor guy, Menken, is locked up and out of the way. That'll help Enzo and his associates make a deal with the Irish."

The door knocker at the funeral home's front entrance banged three times, signaling the arrival of their friend. Roberto walked briskly from the kitchen to open it. As soon as

Trusgnich's bodyguard had determined the interior was free of threats to his boss, he stepped aside for the men to embrace.

Trusgnich smiled slightly, raised his shoulders just a touch, and said, "At least we tried. I sent two guys to stop it. One of them got killed, the other one killed both the Irish, but . . . too late."

"It happens," Roberto told him. "It's water under the bridge. Come on in." Roberto motioned for his old friend and the bodyguard to enter.

# CHAPTER 30

## LUIGI'S

The slabs of black Italian marble framing the front window of Luigi's on the corner of Wilbert and 205th Street, gleamed in the moonlight of a warm summer evening.

The restaurant stood alone in its polished elegance in the midst of a relatively run-down section of the Bronx. Family members of the organized criminal variety in Manhattan financed wedding receptions, baptisms, and First Communion celebrations, as well as the occasional mob conference, in its spacious banquet room in the back. Electronic listening devices were routinely ripped from the light fixtures, inside the light switch plates, and under the tables and chairs, much to the irritation of the owner, Luigi himself. Now the room was taken apart and reassembled weekly, looking for microphones.

A gentle breeze blew off the surface of the reservoir a few blocks away.

It was August 1956. A month ago, Alfred Menken had been convicted of triple murder and had declined to appeal the judgment. Although he'd requested a speedy execution, the powers that be refused to be rushed. It would be a minimum of two years before his death sentence could be carried out.

A party was going on in the banquet room in the back. Giuseppe, the lone waiter in the establishment, in his sixties but appearing much older, wore a black tuxedo and poured the wine. He had seen his share of local color in a lifetime of waiting tables and tending bar. His politeness was derived from years of experience catering to loud, heavily muscled gorillas whose favored sidearms were inadvertently exposed from under their jackets by arm gestures made to support critical points of conversation.

Alice stood and announced to the gathered crowd of guests, "This is my favorite restaurant in the whole world, and you are my favorite people."

She wore a red dress with thin straps and black high-heeled shoes. The visual effect commanded everyone's respectful attention.

Her neighbor, Elaine, sat nearby with her date, Police Detective Andrew Bennett. "Alice, take it easy on the wine. Otherwise, my fiancé will have to arrest you for public intoxication."

Bennett shrugged his shoulders at Elaine. "I'm off duty."

Elaine and Andrew had ice water.

"You're engaged?" Alice responded. "How wonderful. I'm so happy for you both."

Alice continued, "I wanted to thank you all for the help you've given me these last few years. I have no idea what I'm going to do with my life after this. I am a divorced woman who swore to be single for the rest of my life. Now I'm romantically entangled with this man." She pointed to Jim Peters in the chair beside her.

"Furthermore," she went on, "there's the matter of my law degree, due to arrive in the next year. My bosses have asked me to stay with them after I graduate."

Jack Bryce, one of her employers, looked at Alice and smiled. "You can specialize in whatever you want, and we'll support you. You are the best legal assistant we could ever have hoped for. We would love you to think about continuing as our investigator, but we would certainly understand if recent events have diminished your enthusiasm for that kind of work."

Alice smiled happily back at Jack. "If you think I'm going to be intimidated by a little scratch on my arm and a bang on the head, forget it. I'm tough, you know, and I'm not gonna hang it up just because of a little trouble. Besides, I have two impressive gentlemen at my beck and call to protect me, Jim and Antonio."

Jim smiled and raised his hands in surrender. Antonio had not yet arrived.

"I want you all to meet my friends Roberto and Tina, the Cavutos, who are here tonight from down the street. The local funeral home belongs to them. Thank you, Mr. Cavuto, for what you've done for me this summer and the incredible spaghetti dinners you fed us."

"It was nothing, Alice. You've been good company." He raised his wineglass in salutation.

Manny Harrison, the druggist, sat near the Cavutos with his wife.

"And Manny," she spoke to him. He stopped talking to his wife and looked up at Alice. "You have been much more than a neighborhood pharmacist to me."

Manny reddened. He knew Alice would never betray his illicit role as Roberto's assistant during her surgery, and others, under questionable circumstances. He smiled in acknowledgment.

Her law firm's entire partnership was in attendance. They were paying for dinner, and none of them intended to miss an Italian feast. Besides Jack Bryce and his wife, Ivy, there was Jack's original partner, Rich Adams, and Rich's wife, former temporary secretary Mavis Costello, now Mavis Adams. Rich had finally married the woman he had been fooling around with in the stationery closet.

Jack's secretary, Edith Burrows, had become Alice's good friend, and she sat quietly sipping a glass of wine, conversing with her now longtime boyfriend, Eric Fulton.

Clarence Eaton, a new partner at the law firm, sat with his wife.

Freddie Quinn, another possible new partner, was with his wife and the Eatons. Even Eaton's longtime secretary, Laura McDonald, was there with her boyfriend.

"Alice, congratulations," said Franklin Jones from the *Post*. He sat with yet another much younger girlfriend, Janette Monroe, this time brown-haired. "You've given me a lot to write about in the last couple of years. Your maniacal intervention in the garage robbery last year, your masterful handling of Jim's difficulties upstate, the purse snatcher you re-snatched the purse from here in the Bronx, and now, the rise and fall of labor leader Alfred Menken. You got me involved in Menken's shenanigans just in time to see him get nailed. Stay with the firm, Alice. I need material for my column."

"You are very welcome," Alice told him.

"I'm very sorry about my rotten judgment concerning Miss Pinsky. I got her into your inner sanctum, and she betrayed us both. Her flattery blinded me. I won't make that mistake again." He paused and squinted at his latest girlfriend, lost in suspicion. "My apologies."

Alice answered, "If Louis Shaughnessy

hadn't told the police about Cindy, she could have caused you quite a bit more trouble."

Alice's mother, Rose, sat quietly at a table with her sister-in-law, Alice's Aunt Betsy. Rose was enjoying her daughter's friends and the esteem in which they obviously held her. Cousin Fran, Betsy's daughter, sat at that same table with a handsome date in tow.

Once in a while, Alice caught her mother's tearful eye looking at her and giving her daughter an approving smile, reminding them both of the absence of Alice's father, Fred, and Alice's brother, Phil, both gone now. They would have loved this group of people and the measure of success Alice had achieved.

Antonio Vargas and Maria showed up.

"Finally," Alice uttered.

"Please, Miss White. We are just fashionably late. You remember my wife, Maria."

Alice felt herself color. She felt the

heat. She couldn't control it. She did not like that she still had a thing for Antonio. She thought he did for her too. She looked at Maria, who looked back into her eyes. In that moment, Alice knew that Mrs. Vargas was aware of her husband and Alice's mutual attraction but was confident that neither of them would ever act on it. Alice saw that Maria was tough enough to accept it with grace. She was married to Antonio. It was okay with her if he worked up his appetite elsewhere, as long as he dined at home. Alice admired Maria for that and hoped they could be friends.

Antonio gave Alice a steamy glance that bounced off her spine and dropped into her stomach. That accomplished, he turned and shook Jim's hand. "We have to go. We only wanted to say hello to everyone. People are waiting for us downtown."

# CHAPTER 31

## ALICE AND JIM

The heat was unbearable in Alice's apartment, even with both front and rear window fans on maximum speed. Alice climbed out the bedroom window onto the fire escape to get some fresh air. She brought pillows for her and Jim to sit on. She wore the pajama top she had taken from Jim's overnight bag. She liked seeing Jim shirtless and teasing him in his own top.

They sat side by side and gazed out over the southern Italian enclave below.

"Alice," Jim told her, "I never looked so good in that pajama top."

She kissed him on the cheek. “I can tell it excites you.”

“I’m a very patient man,” Jim replied and took a slow, deep breath. “Besides, it is way too hot in there. While I’m waiting to have my way with you, there’s something I want to discuss that we left unfinished at Luigi’s.”

“Ugh, Jim. I was drunk. I don’t remember anything I said.”

“Calm down, Alice. I love the way it is between us. I just want to tell you that I don’t see myself with anyone else. We’ve both been too busy since we met to have anything like a life together. Maybe that’s a good thing, just getting together like this on weekends.”

“Exactly, Jim. And the shock of things changing would probably kill my mother.”

“Alice, you are a riot. That’s a very funny way to put it. You’re a modern woman, and I’m proud to have such a big part in your life. A real man doesn’t need to own a woman to prove to himself that she loves him.”

"Good, Jim, because I do love you. You know I do, but, on the other hand, I really don't think the way I'm treating you is fair, asking you to understand my need for freedom. I'm not even sure I understand it myself. I was not brought up to live this way, single and, yet, carrying on an intimate relationship with a man. I feel guilty. I'm expected to get married, then pregnant, then fat. That's all there's supposed to be in this world for a woman. Especially since the war in Europe and the Pacific ended and the men came home to take back over the country. I'm not saying you didn't deserve to get your jobs back. If it weren't for you, we would all be speaking other languages. You should have been treated special. You risked your lives to protect us all. I just got used to wearing the pants, and I guess I'm having trouble taking them off."

"Please, Alice. Can you try and describe it a little less graphically? I'm not ready to go back inside just yet."

"Okay, Jim. Just for you, I'll refrain

from using that analogy." She batted her eyelashes at him.

"But, seriously," he continued. "I see what you've been up against. You aren't the kind of woman to be put away in the country somewhere to cook and clean and be taken for granted. That doesn't mean I don't still want to own you."

"Oh, God, Jim, what a thing to say. I thought you said you understood me. Where did I go wrong?"

"You went wrong, Alice, when you shook my hand in your boss's office the day we met. You were mine from that moment on, all mine. You just didn't know it."

"Well, geez, where should we live then? Here, in my apartment? Your place in Manhattan? Ugh. You're a difficult man, James. You do understand we'd be living in sin?"

"I find that very exciting, Alice. In fact, it has made me lose my interest in this conversation altogether. We'll talk about where to live when we come back out here later. I changed my mind about the temperature. Let's go inside. We can catch this breeze afterward. Don't be afraid, Alice. I'll be gentle."

"I'm not worried at all, Jim. It is you who should be afraid, very afraid."

# EPILOGUE

Old Sparky

On August 6, 1890, William Kemmler became the first man to be executed in an electric chair, at Auburn Prison in New York. The "chair" was designed by Thomas Edison employees, with the idea it would be a more humane method of execution than hanging. Edison, the pioneer of direct current, or DC, electricity, had his men use alternating currents to stick it to his competitor, the promoter of AC, George Westinghouse. It backfired. The first passage of current through Kemmler failed to kill him, and a rest period of several minutes was required to recharge before they could administer the killing dose of 2,000 volts. Westinghouse famously commented that an ax would have been more humane.

Nevertheless, execution by electrocution in the electric chair became the standard in New York State. On June 19, 1953, Julius and Ethel Rosenberg were executed by this means at Sing Sing Prison for passing atomic secrets to the Soviet Union.

Sing Sing is located in Ossining, New York. Its electric chair was nicknamed "Old Sparky."

On July 10, 1958, two years after his conviction for triple homicide, Al Menken sat on the edge of his bunk in the very same holding cell that had briefly housed the illustrious espionage couple. Menken was the sole inhabitant. He wore denim pants and a denim shirt. The absence of a belt reflected the state's intention not to be denied its due by Menken's premature and, more importantly, unwitnessed, suicide.

Even though he had declined his lawyer's offer to appeal his conviction, it had taken two full years to reach the end of this long—and what he considered inevitable—life journey.

It was getting late. As Menken had expected, there was no word of a pardon or a stay of execution. The only good news for Menken was that he could die only once for the three murders he was convicted of. He was not surprised they had given him the chair. Julius and Ethel Rosenberg might not even have been guilty of the crime they were executed for, but he knew for certain he was guilty of the crimes with which he was charged.

Alfred worked to control his breathing. He intended to die like a man.

A paunchy middle-aged gentleman in a black suit with a white clerical collar appeared outside the cell. Father James O'Brien was the Menken family's parish priest. A guard standing behind the priest reached around him to unlock the cell door.

"Good to see you, my son," Father O'Brien, in his thick Irish brogue, greeted his parishioner. He gripped a bar and swung the cell door open. "You look like you're holding together pretty well. Anna is at home. The doctor has given her a sedative, and her family is with her."

"That's good, Father," Menken told him, maintaining a calm demeanor by force of will. "This is the life I chose, and I've always been willing to pay the price. How is it outside, Jim?"

"Bright and sunny. It's not a bad day to say goodbye to this world and take on the duties of the next. You know, there is something you can do to get right with your Maker before you meet Him."

"Father, don't you think it's a little late for that? I made my bed. Now it's time for me to lie down in it. It's what I know, what I've always known; when you take bad actions, bad things happen to you. I have made my peace with it. You should too."

"I understand what you're saying, Alfred, but I am a man of the cloth, and you might want to humor me, since we are moving out of your area of expertise and into mine. Kneel."

Alfred lifted his hands in surrender and got down on his knees.

"Put your hands together," Father O'Brien instructed him. "Close your eyes, and repeat after me. Our Father, who art in heaven . . ."

An hour later, Menken was on the bunk finishing a steak, a baked potato, and a piece of apple pie. O'Brien was sitting on a straight-backed chair, smoking a cigarette, his legs crossed, his gaze aimed out the small cell window high on the wall, deep in contemplation. Menken wiped his mouth with the cloth napkin provided and dropped it onto the empty dinner plate.

"Not bad," he commented.

Two guards arrived. One unlocked the cell; the other walked in and took Menken's tray. They assumed their places beside the prisoner. Each took an arm. The priest dropped his cigarette on the floor, stepped on it, and led the party into the short corridor to the death chamber.

Inside sat “Old Sparky.” Menken walked calmly to the chair with no help from the guards, who had released his arms in respect for the inmate’s impressive acceptance of his fate. Alfred turned around to face his three escorts and seated himself as if for a haircut. The guards affixed the straps to his arms and legs and then around his chest. There was a window built into the wall in front of the chair, with drapes hung on a rod covering it to obscure the view of the witnesses assembled in the next room until just before the actual execution. No friends or family of either the victims or the condemned man had chosen to attend.

When Menken was securely strapped into the chair, and the electrode was in place on his head, the warden appeared in the doorway, pulled the cord, and drew the curtains open.

“Alfred Aloicious Menken, you have been found guilty of the premeditated murders of three men by a jury of your peers and have been sentenced to death by electrocution. I am here to see that the sentence is carried out. Before I do, is there anything you wish to say to the witnesses assembled?"

"Yeah," Menken spoke up. "I'm not gonna say I'm sorry for what I've done or beg for mercy, 'cause I'm gettin 'what I deserve. Tell Anna she's been a good wife to me, and I appreciate that. Tell my nephew, Philip, and my associate, Louis Shaughnessy, who both ratted me out, that they should, with all due respect, Father, rot in hell. That's all I got to say. Let's get this over with."

Menken's head was secured with a strap across his forehead, and the hood was dropped over his face. The witnesses could be heard moving uncomfortably in their seats, bracing themselves.

The warden pointed a finger at the guard on the switch.

A second later, the loud buzz of arcing electricity filled the execution room and the witness gallery. Pulses rose. Menken strained forward. His hands twitched, his body shook, smoke rose from his clothing; the room filled with the stench of bowel movement, bladder contents, and burnt flesh.

The room went silent. All that was left was the awful smell. Pulses in the gallery began to slow. Menken's had stopped altogether.

**THE END**

# ACKNOWLEDGMENTS

Above all people, I want to thank my wonderful wife, Millie, who believed in me as a writer and gave me time and loving space to create these characters and set them in motion. Her critique was amazing, instructive, and much appreciated. Without you, this book would not have happened.

I owe a debt of gratitude to Kentucky State Police Detective Chad Winn, who was invaluable in his advice concerning my two New York City police detectives and the overall plot of *Hard Case*.

To Tom Pardue of Tom Pardue's East West Kung-Fu Academy in Bowling Green, Kentucky, a warm thanks for reviewing and approving my historical Japanese martial arts material and the use of fighting techniques in my story.

I can never stop thanking my initial writing mentor and role model, Hollywood screenwriter and professor of screenwriting Rich Krevolin, who taught me to write in my favorite reading style, cinematically. He told me I could do this and showed me what it takes to write a compelling story.

In loving memory of my father, Manny Hirsch, the pharmacist I affectionately described in his corner drugstore across the street from the dirty white brick apartment building I grew up in with my older sister, Nancy.

A special thanks to Laura Dragonette who professionally proofread and added a layer of polish I could never have achieved without her.

Finally, to my extended family, friends, and fans, who urged me to keep this up and write into the future, thank you all so much. It helps immensely to compose for a highly prejudiced audience who, I know, already love my work.

# ABOUT THE AUTHOR

Marc Hirsch was born in New York City in 1945. He grew up in the Bronx on the Grand Concourse at 205th Street, in Alice White's dirty white brick building, and walked down the hill, through the southern Italian enclave, to attend the Bronx High School of Science. He graduated from Boston University School of Medicine in 1969.

He moved to California for his postgraduate medical training, then to an island off the coast of British Columbia, back to New York State, and finally to Kentucky, where he retired from medical practice in 2011 and now lives with his wife, Millie.

# OTHER NOVELS BY MARC HIRSCH

**The Con Case: Book 3 in the Alice White Series.**

Daring law firm investigator, Alice White, enters the glamorous world of high society in 1950s New York City to take on a gang of confidence artists whose vicious leader has recruited an innocent young man and framed him for a brutal murder to insure his loyalty. Can she beat the boss at his own game, con him out of a fortune, free the youth, and hang the leader in his own frame, without getting herself, the young man, or his girlfriend killed?

Continue Alice White's adventures and follow her through every twist and turn!

*"Setting and time period are perfect for a fun old fashioned detective story!"* - *Amazon Reviews*

*"Marc has a way of pulling the reader in, and making you feel as though you know Alice personally."*

- *Eugene Madsen*

Made in the USA
Middletown, DE
14 September 2021